Bowtie Mafia

By

Cole Hart

Chapter 1

July 1999 – Atlanta, GA

Tiny drops of water danced on Jaya Woods' body as she stepped out of the walk-in shower. She grabbed a towel, quickly wrapped her hair up, and then stared at herself in the mirror. Standing naked with the door wide open, she posed briefly, idolizing her own body. Her shape was nearly an hourglass, and her skin was smooth and tight. Maybe a couple of shades lighter than milk chocolate. She'd been told over and over as a child that she favored her father, however, as she thoroughly examined herself in the mirror, she knew that she had taken after her mother.

With another thick terry cloth towel, Jaya slowly dried her body off from top to bottom, then placed her hands on her hips, posing as if she was in a photo shoot with Marc Baptiste. She was naturally beautiful. Removing the towel from her head, she set it down on the marble countertop. Jaya loved how the water made her long black hair look silky and sexy, but beauty alone was nowhere near enough to pull off what she was about to attempt in the next twenty-four hours. Although she felt that her plans and mission were foolproof, Jaya still had prepared herself for the worst. Just thinking about making her boyfriend, Santonio, proud of her, shit, just thinking about Santonio alone made her pussy wet and her nipples hard.

Jaya couldn't help reminiscing about how they'd first met as she rubbed vanilla scented Victoria's Secret body lotion over her thick muscular legs.

Jaya made it a ritual to spoil herself at least once a week by shopping at Saks, Neiman Marcus, the Ralph Lauren shop or any other store between Phipps and Lennox. She was a twenty-one year old black woman, who attended Spelman College. Jaya no kids, and between her mother and stepfather, they made nearly a half a million dollars a year. Jaya was an only child, and as such, her parents naturally indulged her. There were no spending limits.

Dressed in hip-hugging denim capri pants, a cute bebe shirt, and a nice pair of four-inch heels, Jaya was definitely the shit as she walked out of one of her favorite shops. Carrying a shopping bag with a nice Dolce and Gabanna suit that she'd just purchased for nearly eight hundred dollars and a pair of Giuseppe heels, she considered the trip to be a rousing success. The fit was a cute yellow linen two-piece that she was going to wear to a private party on Sunday that Jagged Edge was sponsoring along with Jermaine Dupree.

Jaya went straight to her trunk, inserted her key, and opened it. After she put her bags inside and slammed it shut, she stood there for a moment and scanned the parking lot. In a split second, she turned around and headed back toward the mall. She only wanted a small drink, nothing major. Then she changed her mind yet again, turned on her heels and headed back to her car.

Jaya decided to head to Justin's, her favorite spot, off Peachtree. It wasn't too far from Phipps, but in this Saturday traffic, it took her nearly thirty minutes to get there. When she finally arrived, she parked her Lexus Sports Coupe around back. No valet, just a regular parking spot. She got out and made some last minute adjustments to her clothes, which hugged her like a second skin, and triggered her alarm. The young college junior put on her meanest walk and sashayed to the front entrance like she owned the world. Not even Atlanta's hottest weather could keep her from looking her best.

Jaya opened the gold plated doors of the restaurant and was greeted by a handsome and friendly face.

"Welcome to Justin's, Miss Woods! How may I help you this evening?" said a well-groomed maitre'd who looked to be no more than twenty-two years old. He knew that Jaya was a regular customer at the restaurant and had seated her more than four times on separate occasions.

Flashing her beautiful smile, Jaya finally said, "I'll take the bar today." She smirked as she watched his eyes, which stayed glued to her cleavage.

The maitre'd always stared at her in a sexy, but respectful manner, if there was such a thing. All Jaya could do was smile and shake her head. He guided her toward his station first and picked up one of the menus.

"Would you like to browse through the menu, or order today's special, which is the Island Chicken Breast with spicy tomatoes?" the maitre'd asked.

"Umm, sounds good, but right now I'm just trying to have me a tiny drank," Jaya replied as he led her to one of the plush open stools at the bar.

The bar was one of the main attractions at Justin's, besides the chance of bumping into Puffy himself. It was an exquisite, custom crafted bar made from fine cherry oak. Chilling here and having a drink was a lot more comfortable than Pretensions, and that's one of the reasons she enjoyed the bar scene more than occupying a table. Besides, only in this setting, could she sometimes envision herself as the girl in the movie, Cocktail, who flirted with Tom Cruise while sipping on a long island iced tea.

Unfortunately, this bartender was far from Tom Cruise, and her drink of choice was a double shot of Courvoisier XO, just two ice cubes, and a small squeeze of lemon juice. When she ordered her drink, she fanned herself with her hand in a very prissy manner; it wasn't hot, but she was warm. Looking around, she admired for the hundredth time, all the expensive artwork throughout the restaurant.

Business was starting to pick up. Couples were walking in, and jazzy females entered in crews of threes and fours. A couple of guys came in as well. Jaya scanned them quickly and turned her head away. As the bartender brought her drink over, Sade's "Cherish the Day" began to drift through the speakers. He paused in front of her and smiled. She flashed him one back while he placed the glass on a napkin with the Justin's logo engraved in the right hand corner.

Jaya was a little more relaxed now, and she began singing in a low tone along with Sade. The music was coming crisp and clear from the hidden speakers in the walls, and it seemed to wrap itself around her.

Jaya licked her full lips as she guided the glass up to her mouth, preparing herself for the soothing taste of the cognac as it kissed her tongue. She'd been waiting nearly all day to relax and enjoy her drink. It was nearly devoured in two swallows.

Out of the corner of her eye, Jaya noticed a handsome man sitting three barstools down from her. She casually glanced over at him, but then she had to take a second look. Oh my God! She thought to herself. Get it together, Jaya. Setting her glass back on the counter, she took in the scent of his cologne, which was the familiar Jean Paul Gautier, and finally looked at him again. He was a thug; she figured that off the top.

As her eyes scanned the handsome stranger from head to toe, Jaya tried not be too eager. Shit, this nigga fine! She mentioned to herself and sipped her drink again. His well-toned physique was on display in his cocaine white Polo wifebeater that complemented his blue denim shorts. She could even hear her mother's voice whispering in her ear.

Jaya, nine times out of ten, you can always tell a man's character by the shoes he wears.

Well, her mother would have probably been disappointed if she'd let this particular guy get away, because he was wearing a pair of bone white alligator sandals with gold buckles. That definitely said a lot about his character.

Jaya couldn't help it, her eyes scanned him yet again. His demeanor was smooth and nonchalant as he spoke softly, but also in a masculine tone, to the bartender. He glanced over at Jaya and smiled as he waited for his drink. She stared at him this time, impressed with his ivory white teeth. So much so, that she gave him a smile back and slightly turned her body toward him and crossed her legs, to give him more of a reason to stare.

Jaya searched her memory to see if she'd seen him somewhere before. No! There was no way she'd ever encountered him before that day, because she wouldn't have ever forgotten a baby face like his. His eyes were slanted a little, nearly like a Chinese man, and he was wearing lavender tinted Cartier platinum frames. Jaya looked away from him, and just when she was about to take another sip of her drink, he said something that sounded so cool and sexy, she didn't know how to respond.

"Como estas?" he said to her.

That just added fuel to the fire. Never before had Jaya met a man this handsome who spoke Spanish. It had been five, maybe six years since she'd even spoken any damn Spanish herself. He really did catch her off guard with that one, and she definitely wasn't about to pass up the opportunity to respond.

Staring the handsome stranger square in the eyes, Jaya said, "Si! Mi papa es pander."

He laughed at her, and then said, "I like your humorous style already. What's your name?"

"Jaya." She responded arrogantly, trying to figure out the joke that had flown over her head.

He immediately read her tone and body language. "So, I see you feelin' some type of way, huh? I asked 'how are you?' in Spanish, and obviously, you misunderstood me."

"Well, tell me what did I say, mister?"

He extended his hand out to her. Jada gave him her hand, and he brought it to his lips and softly kissed the back of it. Still holding her hand, his eyes went to hers, and he said, "I am Santonio." He was as cool as he could be.

The bartender came back and set the drink down. Santonio cut his eyes at it and then looked up at him. "This is not what I ordered, Tony." His tone turned up a notch. "I asked for a bottle of

Cuvee Dom Perignon 1985, and two glasses. Not a glass of Cuvee."

Tony, the bartender, looked disappointed as he realized he'd messed up the order. He looked down at his notepad for a second and then back at Santonio, then to Jaya, and back to Santonio. "Sorry about that, sir. Give me a minute, okay?"

"And put her drink on my tab, too," Santonio said without taking his eyes off Jaya.

"No problem, sir," he said, and spun on his heels and hurriedly walked away.

Jaya playfully snatched her hand away from Santonio and gave him an 'I can pay for my own drink. Who he think he is?' look.

Tony returned with the champagne bottle sitting in a bucket of ice, and two champagne flutes. He set the bucket in front of Santonio, along with one of the glasses, and then placed the other glass in front of Jaya.

Without a word, Santonio stood up.

Jaya looked up at him as he towered over her, standing every bit of six-foot-three, with wide, bulky shoulders, a low haircut, and a razor-sharp line up like Steve Harvey used to wear before he went to the bald head. Once again, she thought to herself, Damn! This nigga fine as hell!

Santonio softly placed his hand on the upper part of her back, and said to her, "Jaya, did your plans at Justin's have anything to do with meeting me this evening?"

Jaya shrugged and smiled at him. She knew he was a flirt, so she went along with it for the entertainment. "I'm not really sure, Santonio."

"Ooh, you said my name like you were singing a song. How about joining me at the table? I'm dolo, you dolo. That is ... unless you are waiting for someone else."

With his last sentence, she realized that he was a slick talker. She couldn't believe her ears, but it was amusing to hear.

"I am waiting on somebody." She lied to him just as smooth as he was talking. Hmph, trying me like a Freak-a-leek trick or something, she said to herself.

"Are you serious?"

"I'm only teasing! I'd love to take you up on your offer," Jaya said, nibbling on her bottom lip in a seductive manner. She slightly turned on the stool and stood up; collecting her belongings just as the maitre'd was coming in their direction.

Santonio grabbed Jaya's hand. She looked up at him and smiled. For some reason, she was slightly nervous.

He looked at the bartender before they walked off, and handed him a folded one hundred dollar bill. "Bring my champagne and glasses over to the table for me," Santonio said.

Tony's eyes were happy. He grabbed the bucket and the glasses while Santonio led Jaya through the restaurant behind the maitre'd.

When they reached the table, Santonio asked the maitre'd, "Can you get a particular song on for me?"

"Sure, which one?"

Santonio turned toward Jaya, looked her in the eyes for a second, and then looked back at the man. "Wild Flower, by New Birth."

The maitre'd nodded in agreement as the bartender placed the glasses and bucket of champagne on the table.

Santonio pulled out Jaya's chair and stood behind her while she scooted up to the table. Just then, another waiter came out with two glasses of water. Jaya sat quietly, taking everything in. She noticed that other beautiful women were watching her and Santonio, as if she wasn't good enough to be with a man that sexy and fine.

Santonio sat down across from her, removed the bottle of champagne from the bucket of ice, and popped the cork. Jaya sat there watching him, her eyes twinkling. She was trying to hold her composure; didn't want to seem too thirsty.

As he poured up their glasses, the song came through the hidden speakers. Santonio flashed a smile immediately. The tone was set. He lifted his flute and held it out toward Jaya.

Jaya lifted her flute and touched it to his. "So, where did you get a name like Santonio from?"

Santonio put his lips on the gold rim of the glass and turned it up a little. Sipping on the cold champagne was refreshing to him. Then he said to Jaya in a casual tone, "It's funny because people ask me that all the time. My name was given to me by my mother. She named me after her father."

"So your grandfather's name is Santonio as well? Okay, that name fits you, even though you're more of a pretty boy. Santonio sounds thuggish."

Santonio almost spit champagne from his mouth when she made that comment.

"Pretty Boy? Thuggish?" He said and released a chuckle while shaking his head. "God bless the dead. My mom used to call me the same thing."

Jaya's facial expression turned a little serious. "What happened to your mother?"

Santonio removed the bottle from the ice bucket, poured some more into his glass, and held the bottle up to see if Jaya wanted any more. She held up her glass and he topped her off, eased the bottle back into the bucket, and then said to her, "My mom passed away two years ago." He looked down at his right arm and rubbed his portrait tattoo.

Jaya could feel every bit of that energy. Her eyes went back up to his, and she said, "My dad was killed when I was five years old. Then my mother married this clown, who I sooo can't stand ... Ughhh!" Jaya paused and sipped her champagne, thinking about her childhood. It was time to change the subject. Looking down at the tiny bubbles trapped in her champagne flute, she continued, "But enough about me. My life is kinda boring. What's going on with you?" She reached across the table and removed his Cartier shades from his face. His eyes were bronze and sexy. She put them on her face and tried to mimic him.

Santonio nodded approvingly at her; he was checking her style, and she was definitely cool. "I do a lot of shit, actually. I came out here from Arizona with about a hundred thousand dollars. I opened up a record store and started burning CDs and club promoting, mainly with local rappers, you know? Then I do a couple more things on the side to keep my revenue coming in."

"Sounds like you're a very busy man, and definitely interesting, to say the least."

"It's cool, especially when you can kick it with some of your favorite rappers. But it can be a headache sometimes too. Me, personally, I need a vacation sometimes. All work and no play can lead you to make bad business decisions from time to time, you know?"

Santonio slowly nodded his head to the soothing sounds of New Birth; the music was like a soul soother for him. He picked up his glass again, put it to his nose, closed his eyes, and inhaled the aroma of his favorite champagne.

"What you got planned for tomorrow, Jaya?" he asked.

"I'll be going to a private Jagged Edge party, hosted by Jermaine Dupree. It's definitely gonna be off the chain, and I been waiting a while for this. I love them for real."

Santonio listened to Jaya for a moment, and then he moved his champagne glass over toward her. "Let's toast to our new beginning." His voice was smooth and charming.

Jaya raised her glass up to his.

"Tomorrow, we'll go down to Miami, walk the beach, eat, shop, and relax."

Jaya's smile faded. "Excuse me, but didn't you hear me say that I'm going to the Jagged Edge party? Sorry, but no Miami for me, sir." Jaya shook her head. She couldn't believe that he was actually trying her like that. This nigga must be crazy. She thought.

With a half-hearted laugh, Jaya sipped her champagne again. "Puh-leez, dude."

Chapter 2

Jaya and Santonio arrived at Miami International at a little after 11:00 AM the next morning. Santonio had been a little more persuasive than Jaya thought he would be, and she was feeling him a bit, so she didn't have a problem changing her mind. Santonio had everything planned out perfectly for them. It was only a two-day trip, and all he needed from her was her company to make him look good. Jaya was a dresser, and she loved attention.

Santonio looked toward her as the plane finally came to a halt. Jaya was looking out the window, lost in thought. "I'll assume that you've never been to Miami."

Jaya turned her head, snapping out of her thoughts. "No, never been to South Florida. I went to Disney World when I was younger, though.

Santonio took her hand, wedged his fingers between hers, and said, "Well, let me tell you a little something about Miami from my point of view. It's very relaxing, and clearly a city for lovers." He squeezed her hand and looked seductively into her eyes.

Jaya's eyes turned glossy; he had her mind spinning out of control now. She looked him up and down and thought he looked even better today than yesterday. Dressed in a comfortable looking white linen suit with a pair of matching Louis Vuitton boat shoes on, he truly looked like a man of means. The two big five-carat diamond earrings sparkling from each earlobe only enhanced his image. With that said, all she could do was smile at him and shake her head.

Twenty minutes later, they were leaving the airport in a glossy black double stretch Lincoln Navigator. Inside, Santonio had arranged to have a dozen white roses spread over the leather interior. He definitely knew how to set the tone and lay it out for a woman. Then Santonio pressed a button and opened the sunroof just above their head. The breeze flowed through, giving then both a more relaxed feeling. The chemistry was definitely there. Santonio stood unexpectedly, put his head out the sunroof, and yelled, "I think I found my soulmate, everybody!"

Jaya was smiling and looking up at him with an embarrassed expression. *Is he serious right now?* She thought to herself. Santonio repeated himself again and again as they rode through

Miami. The smile on her face was enormous and very much authentic.

When he finally came back down and sat next to her, he leaned toward her and kissed her passionately. His tongue went inside her mouth and she French kissed him back. He pulled away from her and began to sing, "Meet me at the altar in your white dress. We ain't getting' no younger girl, so we might as do it." He paused the song and kissed her again. Then he held on to her for a moment as they rode in silence.

On South Beach, they went to a nice elegant spot called LA Café, an Oceanside restaurant. It was a popular dining spot that sold everything from Asian to Cajun Cuisine. Jaya ordered the jumbo shrimp and crab cake rolls with a delicious garden salad. Santonio ordered the same bottle of Cuvee Dom Perignon 1985, and a Cuban dish that Jaya couldn't pronounce. He looked up at her and said, "It's roasted pulled pork." Then he poked out with his fork while Jaya frowned at him.

"I don't eat pork," she stated, then slowly bit into one of the crab cakes. Her eyes fixed on him, watching him eat.

When he finished chewing, Santonio responded, "Well, I guess this is my last time eating it too."

"Oh really?" she said with laughter in her voice.

Santonio and Jaya talked and enjoyed each other for another hour or so; he wanted to know more about her, and she wanted to know more about him.

Outside, the driver of the limousine was sitting behind the wheel with his window rolled halfway down. He was a Spanish looking guy with black eyes, clean shaven, and wore his hair slicked to the back. From the rearview mirror, he saw a yellow taxi pull up behind him. The driver stepped out, walked around the rear of the taxi and opened the trunk. The limo driver watched him as he came out with a box shaped suitcase. He closed the trunk shut, and as he was coming around the cab, the limousine driver pressed a button to open the rest of the limousine. Without a word being exchanged, the taxi driver, an older looking black guy with nappy hair, eased the suitcase into the back of the limousine and politely closed the door. He gave the thumbs up sign to the driver, and went back to the taxi, hopped in the driver seat, and pulled off just as quickly as he arrived.

Back inside the restaurant, Jaya was smiling at Santonio, staring into his intoxicating eyes. "Yes, I'm an AKA, and I'm very proud of it."

Santonio had his cell phone sitting on the table in front of him. The screen illuminated, and his eyes went down to it. He held up a finger to Jaya. "Excuse me for a second," he apologized as he picked up the phone. "Yes," he spoke into his phone.

From the other end, a voice said, "Everything is in place."

"One." Santonio said and hung up. He set the phone back on the table and looked at Jaya. "I got us a room at the Fontainebleau. You wanna get some rest, or you wanna go walking on the beach first?"

"I don't know, what do you think?" She sipped her champagne while giving a devilish, seductive look. She was feeling a bit tipsy, and before he could respond, she said, "Hotel."

Jaya caught Santonio by surprise with that one, but he wasted no time spotting the waiter. He raised his hand. "Check, sir."

———————

At the Fontainebleau hotel, Santonio had a suite reserved for him and Jaya on the 18th floor, with a beautiful view of the city of Miami. Nearly three hours had passed since they'd landed. Inside the bedroom, Jaya lay on top of the sheets in a pair of black boy shorts and a halter top. When Santonio came out of the bathroom, he was in a pair of black Armani boxer briefs, no shirt, no socks. Jaya looked at him as he approached the bed where she lay, staring at his bulge below his waist.

Always a smart one, Jaya produced a condom. He climbed in the bed next to her, and within a few minutes, their bodies were intertwined. Santonio had his mouth on her breast; he could feel the warmth of her breath on his neck, as he entered her. She was warm, wet and tight, like an Isotoner leather glove. For the next hour, he fucked her so good that nothing else mattered to her, but for him, he could only think about the ten kilos of cocaine that he had just scored. Now he was ready to get back to Atlanta, with the perfect woman for the job.

After he had made her cum three times, he laid on top of her; she had her arms around his neck.

The only thing she said was, "Promise me you won't leave me."

Chapter 3

Jaya's two bedroom condo in mid-town was beginning to look like a tornado had come through and ransacked her place. She'd pulled nearly every piece of clothing she owned from her closet to find the right outfit to wear. She paraded around with nothing on but a burgundy silk Kimono that Santonio had bought her a couple of weeks back. Jaya's hair had finally dried, and after she had given it a quick style, she looked at herself in the mirror. She was satisfied with it, but she still was running around like a pit bull puppy looking for its toys.

Jaya was jittery and anxious, thinking to herself that a drink would relax her. Instead, she grabbed the remote, aimed it at her sound system, and Maxwell's voice came at her with the song, "Fortunate." She was in the groove immediately, slow dancing in her closet with herself. Jaya finally got dressed in a stylish business suit, and she hit herself with some Hanae Mori perfume.

Back at the mirror, she studied her reflection again. She was lost in thought for a moment, thinking about the what-ifs. Her mother flashed through her mind, the words slicing straight through her. *Don't be weak hearted or weak minded for no man, Jaya.* She replayed those words repeatedly in her head, and then she picked up on Maxwell's voice again, finding her groove and forgetting what her mother said. When Jaya picked up her watch, it read, 8:44 AM. She strapped it on her wrist, knowing Santonio was serious about being punctual.

"He said he'd be here at nine," she whispered.

Then the phone rang. "Hello?"

"Hey, it's me, baby. I'm outside."

She smiled, feeling relaxed and anxious all at the same time. Then she said into the phone, "Okay, I'm on the way." She hung up the phone, looked at the suitcase that sat next to the couch on the floor.

Jaya turned off the lights in the living room and was headed toward the door when she said, "Shit!" and ran to the bedroom. "Where did I put it?" She asked herself. Jaya switched on the bedroom light at the head of her queen-sized bed and lifted her mattress. "Damn! I just had it."

She got down on her knees and looked underneath the bed. Her eyes scanned around, but still she couldn't find what she was looking for. She searched under her pillows, went to her leather handbag, and dumped all of its contents out. Then her phone rang again. That frustrated her, but she answered it anyway. "Hello."

"I forgot to tell you, you forgot your driver's license in the car."

Jaya closed her eyes for a moment and took a deep breath. She was relieved; it was the fake ID that she was just looking for. When she took trips for Santonio, the name she used was Mrs. Shanice Brooks, and with her new identity, she was a married housewife, six months pregnant, with a husband in the Marines.

"Okay, baby, I'm on the way now."

Santonio and Jaya drove a rental car to the airport. The early morning traffic on Interstate 285 was congested. Cars were creeping at a slow pace, bumper to bumper. An accident had occurred about two miles up ahead. They rode in silence for a few minutes. Santonio was in his own world, all he had on his mind was making sure that Jaya made it back safely with the ten kilos of cocaine that she was about to pick up. By the time they'd gotten closer to the accident, he noticed that it wasn't anything major. A minor fender bender. The only thing that had the traffic moving slowly was the people passing by in their cars being nosey as hell. He slapped the steering wheel with his opened hand after checking the clock. He was getting frustrated. Jaya could not miss her flight.

"Calm down, boo," she said in a soothing tone.

She stared at him, her eyes moving up and down his body. She'd fallen flat on her face for him, and there was nothing anyone could tell her different. When he took a quick glance at her, the most her could do was force a smile and look back at the road.

On the two was a heated discussion about Master P and Pastor Troy, that wasn't important to either of them. The Camp Creek Parkway exit was just ahead. Jaya noticed, but she was thinking about marriage, her and Santonio, finishing college; her future. What would it be like?

"Wuss wrong, baby?" Santonio asked her.

She quickly snapped her head toward him. "Oh, oh nothing. I was just thinking about something."

"Nothing, and you was thinking about something? That don't sound right, Jaya," he responded.

They were both looking straight ahead now. Santonio was switching lanes. They'd passed the accident, and the traffic flow had opened up when she said, "I just love you, and I don't want anything to happen."

Santonio was smooth as they come, real calm and apologetic. He leaned over toward her, still with his eyes on the road. "Give me a kiss."

She leaned over to him, gave him a quick kiss on his lips and he sat back in his driver's position. "I stand on my word, Jaya," he finally said. There was a long pause before he went on. "Do you realize how much I love you?"

She looked at him, her eyes turning moist and sad. Jaya's emotions were confused. Then she nodded her head. "I do."

Santonio took a deep breath, and said, "Listen, Jaya ..." His demeanor was smooth, almost like a slow R&B song. "Everything I'm doing is for us. Not me, but us as one. You may feel a lil uncomfortable about going down to Miami alone, and that's understandable. But I've arranged for you to pick up and be on the first thing smoking out of there tomorrow, okay?"

"Okay."

"You're picking up ten keys, easy money. Look in the glove box and get that envelope."

She opened the glove compartment, removed the fat sealed envelope. She looked over at him, then he said, "It's ten grand in there, go shopping while you there. Get you something to wear."

Jaya dropped the money into her handbag, which was on the floor between her legs. Five minutes later, they were moving up to the Delta section of Hartsfield-Jackson International. The traffic was congested with limousines, cabs, shuttle buses and pedestrians moving in every direction on foot.

Santonio whipped the car in front of the Delta section and blocked off an elderly couple who seemed to be struggling with their luggage. After he put the car in park, he jumped out and helped them with their two big suitcases up to the entrance doors of the airport.

Jaya watched him, even more impressed by his kind spirit. She was stepping out of the car as he was coming back. He came around the nose of the car to her side and wrapped his arms around her waist. Rising up on her tiptoes, she kissed him passionately on his lips. Jaya's heartbeat sped up, then she said, "I love you so damn much," and buried her face in his chest.

"I love you too, baby." He shot back. "Now you remember everything I told you, right?"

She nodded; her eyes bright and alert. When he released her, he went to the back seat and pulled out her carry-on bag, which was filled with over a hundred-thousand dollars in cash, and her suitcase. She carried the carry-on bag, and he carried the suitcase. After one more kiss at the entrance, he waved her off and hoped for the best.

Chapter 4

An hour and a half later, Jaya watched the Miami skyline, as the plane prepared to land. A petite stewardess walked up the aisle with a small trash bag, collecting the plastic cups and other miscellaneous trash. She looked at Jaya and smiled as she was putting a plastic cup into the bag. "Did you enjoy your flight?"

"I did," Jaya said politely as she put a Robb Report magazine in her bag.

The Miami heat blanketed her immediately when she stepped out of Miami International. Florida was a hot state, but Miami was the hottest city. Standing on the curb with her bags, she was still buzzing from the Tanqueray and Sprite that she'd had about forty minutes before. She slipped on a pair of Gucci shades just as a cab eased up.

The driver rolled the passenger side window down and leaned over to look at Jaya. "Need a cab, ma'am?" he asked.

She smiled and nodded, "Yes, please."

The Cuban was a short man with salt and pepper hair. He got out and hurried around to the curb where she stood, grabbed her luggage, and carefully put it in the back seat and closed the door. Jaya hopped in the back seat, and from there, they went to the Fontaine-Bleu Hotel on Collins Avenue. She had reserved a beachfront ocean view suite on the 15th floor.

Once she was settled in her room, Jaya called Santonio from her cellphone. It rang four times before he answered it. "Hello, beautiful, you made it safely?"

She smiled, as she stood at the window. "Yes, baby, I made it safely. It's hot as the world down here. I'm about to take me a shower and relax. Should I be looking for a call or something?"

"Yeah, from me. I'll hit you back when they on the way, okay."

"Okay, love you, boo."

"Love you too, beautiful," he said and hung up.

Jaya ended her call and placed the cell phone on the stand, still looking out the window at the beautiful view. She thought about her mother and picked her phone up to call her.

The first thing here mother said was, "Where are you?"

Jaya rolled her eyes and took a deep breath before responding, "I'm in Miami, Mom."

"Miami?" She nearly shouted. "You were just down there two weeks ago, Jaya. What do you have going on that's so important down there?"

"We've been doing too much arguing lately. I think that you've forgotten that I'm a grown woman now." She turned away from the window, walked over to the bed, and sat down. Just then, her mother said, "You're right." Then the line went dead.

Jaya caught an instant headache. She kicked off her shoes and stretched out on the bed, and within fifteen minutes, she was out cold and deep in dreamland.

In her dream, she was flipping the channels using the remote. She paused on the cartoon channel, where the Road Runner was on. She loved the Road Runner and was more than fascinated by how the Coyote could never catch him. She looked over at her mother; she was scanning over some paperwork for her job. Jaya said to her, "Mommy, we supposed to be watching cartoons together."

Karen never looked up from the paperwork, but she spoke softly to her daughter. "I'll join you in a few. What are you watching?"

Jaya got up on her elbows, with eyes glued to the TV. She said, "The Road Runner. The Coyote is never gonna catch him. He's smart like you."

Karen smiled. "He's smart like you too."

Jaya heard her, but she never responded because she heard the keys at the front door. Her eyes got wide. She looked at her mother. "My daddy home!" She hurried out the bed, climbed down and ran to the bedroom door.

Jaya twisted the knob and pulled the door opened, only to be faced with two men dressed in suits and bowties, like they were going to a wedding. Their faces were covered with pantyhose, and they both held guns in their gloved hands. Jaya looked up at them and noticed that neither of them was her daddy. She stood there, afraid to move, the strange men looked scary. Jaya peed her pants.

One of the men picked her up and spun her around, then put the gun to her head and said to her mother, "We came for the money. Your husband sent us and told me to tell you he loves y'all."

Jaya woke up sweating, her eyes wide with fear. She glanced around the room, unsure of where she was, and then she remembered everything. Tears filled her eyes, just thinking about how they were robbed at gunpoint by two men at her home when she was young. Her father was dead, but his body was never found. She didn't know the full story, only what her mother told her, and that wasn't much.

Growing up, Jaya had tried not to think of that horrible night, and how she and her mother had sat tied up and gagged for nearly two days before anyone found them. The ordeal had affected Jaya's entire childhood and still impacted her life to this day. Her mother had enrolled her in a private school and she'd gone to counseling twice a week. As she got older, she kept herself immersed in school work to keep the horrible memory in the back of her mind. When her mother landed a job in Atlanta, paying nearly a hundred and fifty thousand dollars a year, they were on the first thing smoking out of Augusta.

Jaya got out the bed, looked at her watch. It was nearly 5:00 PM. She got naked, went into the bathroom and turned on the shower. It didn't take her long to wake up under the warm water, and after fifteen minutes, she was out and dressed. As she applied the last of her makeup, the phone rang.

"Hello?"

"Hey! Jaya, listen, a young lady is about to come your way. You already know the rest."

"Any specific time?"

"Within the next hour. Call me back tonight." He said and disconnected the call.

Damn! Jaya said to herself and looked at the phone. By the time she went back to the window, there was a knock at her door. She went to the door, looked through the small peephole and saw a cute faced female standing on the other side. She had to be the girl that Santonio was talking about. Without asking who it was, she unlocked the door and opened it.

The Kelly Rowland lookalike smiled at Jaya. "Hey, I'm Baby Girl," she said and extended her hand.

Jaya shook her hand. "I'm Shanice." She lied smoothly, using her alias. "Come on in."

Jaya checked out Baby Girl as she stepped inside. Her body was exceptionally nice; her stomach was flat, she had nice hips, and a soft round ass that jiggled every time she walked. She was dressed in a summer blouse and fitting linen pants with low heels.

Baby Girl looked around the room and said, "You know what? I'm from Miami, born and raised, and I've never been to this hotel before."

"What?" Jaya said in a surprised tone. This is my third time here, and I love it."

They stood next to each other in silence for a moment, contemplating the gorgeous view. Baby Girl turned to Jaya. "Where you from?"

"Georgia," she said. "I'm living in Atlanta."

"Oh, you a peach," she responded with a smile, and then added, "I've danced up there in Atlanta a couple times. A club called Magic City, you familiar with it?"

"I've never been, but I've heard stories about it," Jaya said. "So, you still dance?"

"Off and on, actually I got one more year at the University of Miami. My sugar daddy don't want me to dance at the Rolex no more because he's a little jealous, you know."

"I definitely know how that goes. So, you at Miami. That's funny because I have one more year at Spelman myself."

"Girl, that's what's up!" Baby Girl checked her watch. She was wearing a white leather band Audemars Piguet with sparkling diamonds in the face. She looked back up at Jaya. "I heard you wanted to go shopping."

"Yeah, I need to pick up a few things."

"Well, we can make that happen. Make sure you bring the money out to the car. That way, when we hit the mall, and you bring your shopping bags up, you can bring your work back up with you. I got them ten keys waiting for you."

Jaya nodded and looked over at the bed. The money was there, untouched. Then she looked back at Baby Girl. "I'm ready."

Chapter 5

Santonio lived in a half million dollar estate in a high class luxury neighborhood called Guilford Forest in the city of Atlanta. Inside his bedroom, he lay on a king sized canopy bed with his girlfriend. They were both naked and lying skin to skin. Shannon was her name. She was in her early thirties, from the Virgin Islands, dark chocolate and cute as a button. Shannon was a tennis player, not a pro or anything like that; she just liked the sport because it kept her body in good shape like Serena Williams.

She rolled over on her side, facing Santonio, and rubbed her hand across his chest, her nails playfully clawing at him. "What's on your mind?" she asked him. "Looks like you're worried about something."

"I just hope shawty make it back safely with them ten, I can't afford another loss."

She kissed Santonio softly on his lips; he kissed her back and was instantly relaxed. Between kisses, she said, "She'll be all right."

Santonio pulled her on top of him; she was soft and warm. Shannon grabbed his dick immediately and guided it inside her. She felt his throbbing dick spreading her walls and placed her hands flat on his chest as she began to rotate her hips. Santonio liked how she fucked because she always came fast. He gripped her ass cheeks, pushed her down on him, and brought her back up, meeting her movement every time. He pushed his dick to the side as he entered, touching her sensitive spot. He watched her eyes roll to the top of her head and her entire body began to tremble from her hands to her toes.

When Santonio felt her thick cum coating his dick, he smiled and flipped her over on her back, pushed her legs back, and slid in and out of her with ease. He put the toes of her right foot in his mouth and pumped deep inside of her until she came again and again. She was sweating now and trying to smile, but the pain was real that he was putting down on her and it made her frown every time he pushed deep. "I feel it in my stomach," she said in a low whisper.

Santonio smiled and pushed himself further inside of her until she screamed out in pain, then came the tears of joy.

After they finished, Shannon climbed out of bed, wrapped herself up in a silk Versace robe, then went into the bathroom. A moment later, she came back with a hot, soapy washcloth and washed Santonio up real good while he laid on his back with his head propped up on the pillows. When his cell phone rang, he answered it on the third ring.

"Hey, baby. I got everything, but I'm gonna drive back."

He frowned. "Drive back? Why?"

"For some reason, Baby Girl said the other outlet wasn't official."

Santonio rubbed his hands over his face. He was confused, but he didn't lose his composure. After a long deep breath, he said, "Do you need me to fly down?"

"Trust me, baby, I can handle it. I'm pulling out in the next thirty minutes, and I'll call you when I get to north Florida, okay?"

"Okay, baby."

"Love you."

His eyes cut down to Shannon. She was slowly cleaning him and kissing the head of his dick. Then he said, "Love you too and drive safe. Do the speed limit." He hung up and tossed the phone to the floor next to him.

Shannon looked up at him and said, "Baby, when you tell her you love her, you should put more emotion into it so she'll believe you."

———————

Nearly fifteen hours had passed, and when Jaya walked into her apartment, Santonio was sitting on the sofa with his legs crossed, reading a USA Today newspaper. He lowered the paper when she walked in and looked straight at her.

Jaya set her bags down at the door. She was tired and drained, but still managed a smile. "I made it," she said as she closed the door.

Santonio got up and went to her. When she turned around and faced him, he wrapped his arms around her and kissed her, then said, "We made it."

Her arms went around his neck. It felt so good to be back in his arms that nothing else mattered. I'm tired," she whispered.

He pecked her lips and then her forehead. "Get you some rest, baby, and let me handle this business. Okay?"

"Okay..." She took off her shoes and walked into her room.

Santonio picked up the suitcase and her carry-on duffle bag. He checked the locks to make sure the door was secure, and then returned to the sofa. He cleared the coffee table, set the suitcase down, and opened it. When he removed the clothes and spring water bottles, there was the first square brick wrapped up neatly in gray duct tape. He picked it up, put it to his nose, and closed his eyes with a look of pure satisfaction. After that, he stacked all ten bricks on the table in two rows of five, and just stared at them for several minutes. It was a big accomplishment on his behalf; ten bricks of A-1 cocaine that belonged all to him. Now he was thinking of his process. He could easily stretch the dope and turn ten to fifteen, or he could go ahead and let them go as is, and double his money on a quick flip.

Santonio took a deep breath and rubbed his hands together. *Damn! My next move,* he said to himself, and then he stood up, picked up one of the bricks and walked into the kitchen. He laid it down on the counter top and removed a sharp kitchen knife from the knife holder. Using the steak knife, he cut a small section through the tape, plastic and grease that it was wrapped in. The strong odor of cocaine hit his nose and he shivered a little. Then he stuck his fingernail in it, pushed a little bit under his pinky nail, brought it to his nose and sniffed one hard time until it disappeared. "We on," he whispered. "Grade A."

A cordless phone sat in its cradle next to where he stood. He picked it up and dialed a number.

A deep voice came into his ear. "Yooo ..."

"Five or ten?" Was all Santonio said.

The guy recognized the voice and caught on to what he was saying immediately. "Ten."

Santonio smiled and gave him instructions as to where to meet him at. They talked for five minutes, and the deal was sealed. Santonio knew how to move and conduct street business without having too many people in his affairs. Within the next three hours, he'd got off all ten bricks of coke and profited an easy one hundred thousand dollars.

When Jaya woke up, she looked around her bedroom and noticed that ten dozen red roses surrounded her room. Then, there were several candles lit. Jaya couldn't believe what she was seeing. Her heart melted and she was nearly in tears. She looked to her left just as the door opened. Santonio entered, no shirt, muscles rippling. He wore an apron around his waist and carried two-half filled champagne glasses.

"I got class today, baby," she said in a low whisper.

"Fuck class," he said as he kissed her lips. When he pulled back away from her, he held up his champagne glass.

"To what, this time?" She touched her glass against his.

"To success and loyalty, baby."

They both shipped from their glasses, then Santonio took both of the glasses and set them on the nightstand. He got completely naked and stood in front of her. Jaya was amazed, and in turn, she got naked herself. She put her hands on his waist and slowly kissed his stomach, then she went down and put him in her mouth. Santonio looked down at her and placed his hand on the back of her head. Her mouth was wet and hot. *Just like her pussy,* he thought.

She cut her eyes up at him. "You like it?" She asked with her mouth full.

He pushed himself deeper into her throat. "I love it, baby."

It did feel good to him, but in reality, he only needed her for her services, and that was strictly to move his cocaine from city to city and state to state. He pushed her backward. She laid back and smiled then instantly spread her legs. Her vagina was waxed and smooth. Santonio put his face between her legs and carefully sucked and licked her in all the right places.

Jaya's entire body trembled. She grabbed the back of his head and started rotating her hips, pushing her pussy in his face. She felt his tongue crawling and touching spots that she never knew existed. Then she felt herself about to cum. Her legs started shaking even more. "Oh my God! It feels so good, baby!" She whispered then lost herself, closed her eyes and allowed her thick cum to gush out.

Santonio crawled up on her and folded her legs back. He pushed himself hard and deep inside of her, to the point that she could do nothing but gasp from the pain.

For the next few hours, Santonio fucked her good and from every position. She was tired and worn out. The whole time they were having sex and fun, Santonio told her that she needed to go back to Miami ASAP. Without hesitation, she was on the next flight.

Chapter 6

The following night, Jaya was back in Miami. This time, she was sitting in the VIP section of the Rolex strip club where Baby Girl worked. There were several beautiful women around in heels and skimpy thongs. Most of them had thick thighs and fat round asses with firm looking breasts.

Baby Girl was wearing a two-piece white lace set and Louboutins. She came into the VIP section where Jaya was sitting on a leather sofa next to a little guy with long dreads and a mouth full of gold teeth. He was charcoal black, with red veined eyes, and huge gold and diamond pieces on his neck, wrist and fingers. Baby Girl leaned down and kissed him on his cheek. "Thanks for picking up my home girl from the airport," she said.

He waved her off. "No problem," he said in his Haitian accent, "she cool."

Baby Girl smiled and sat on the sofa next to Jaya, giving her a quick hug. "I'll be ready in thirty minutes," she said.

"Take your time, I'm good."

Jaya scanned the room and caught a glimpse of an NBA basketball player. "Isn't that the guy who plays for the Atlanta Hawks?" she asked Baby Girl.

Baby Girl didn't seem impressed at all. She actually wasn't paying him any attention. The Rolex was a club that kept major ballplayers and celebrities, and even more hood rich cats. She looked at Jaya. "Yeah, you wanna meet him?"

Jaya smiled; she definitely wasn't ready for that response. "Are you serious? Hell yeah!"

"Give me a second," Baby Girl said and stood up. She sashayed directly over to the baller. "My home girl would like to meet you."

The NBA player stood every bit of six-foot-six, and he knew Baby Girl personally. She was a popular dancer in Miami, and her name held tremendous weight. When he looked down at her, he said casually, "Now, Baby Girl, you know I'm not interested in no groupies."

Baby Girl folded her arms across her chest. "Nigga, you better come over here and meet my homegirl. She from the A, she just wanna meet you."

He turned his head and looked over to where Jaya was sitting. Not only did he see her smiling at him, but he also noticed the mean looking dread sitting next to her, staring in his direction. He nodded his head one time, letting him know that everything was cool. He looked at Baby Girl. "What's her name?"

"Shanice."

He walked in Jaya's direction, and as he went toward her, she stood up. She was holding her composure with a straight face. *Oh my God, he's coming,* she said to herself.

The baller reached out toward her and wrapped her up in his arms, giving her a warm hug. "Hello," he said in a professional manner.

"Hiya doing?" she replied and separated from him. Looking up into his eyes, she asked him, "You still play for the Hawks?"

He nodded, looking down at her all the while. She looked empty, lost, worried. Then he asked her, "You don't look like you belong here. Like something is bothering you."

Jaya gave him her hand, and in a cold tone, she said, "Nice to meet you." She turned and went back to the sofa and sat down next to the dread.

The tall NBA player just looked at her for a brief moment. He half smiled and shook his head before he turned and started talking to a tall yellow female who looked Brazilian.

Jaya ordered herself a drink while she watched a long-legged, exotic dancer give the dread a lap dance. The dread ordered a cold bottle of Cristal, and when the half-naked female waitress brought it, she had a lavender Bowtie around her neck.

Jaya noticed that, if she didn't notice anything else. Her mind immediately flashed back to when the two men came in on her and her mother. Jaya was crying again, they were wrapping her wrist with duct tape. She remembered her mother saying, "Please don't hurt my daughter. Please don't hurt my daughter."

They were calm as could be, Jaya remembered. She could see their Bowties and their suits. Then, she said through tears, "I'ma tell my daddy."

One of the men responded, "He already dead. What he gonna do?"

"Jaya," Baby Girl said for the second time, snapping her out of her daydream. She was fully dressed and standing before her with a big leather Gucci bag on her shoulder.

"You ready?" Jaya asked.

"Yep, let's get out of here."

Jaya stood up, and the dread stood up with her. "Yawl good?" he asked them.

Baby Girl gave the dread a warm embrace, and so did Jaya. "Yeah, we good, sweety," Baby Girl said, and then she and Jaya found their way to the parking lot.

Baby girl was driving a hot pink Corvette convertible. The top was already down, and the huge bouncer that stood next to it had been paid just to personally watch her car. He watched Baby Girl as she approached the driver's side. Jaya went to the passenger's side, admiring the car, enjoying the cool Miami breeze.

Baby Girl handed the huge, mean looking guy three hundred dollars. She briefly hugged him and said, "I'm gone for the night."

He nodded. "I'm out here."

Baby Girl opened her door and hopped in while Jaya was climbed into the passenger side. The interior of the Corvette was cocaine white and soft leather. She was impressed when Baby Girl started the car, and the loud sound system came on as well. The female rapper, Trina, came from the speakers and Baby Girl got turnt up instantly.

They were enjoying themselves so much when they pulled out the parking lot, that they never noticed that they were being followed by the Feds.

Chapter 7

When Baby Girl arrived at her estate in North Miami, Jaya was in total shock. The house was a five-bedroom mansion that looked like it belonged on the cover of a magazine. She looked at Baby Girl as she punched her security code in the pad. The gate opened, and Jaya couldn't help but to ask, "You live here by yourself?"

Baby Girl glanced over at Jaya. She pressed a button, and the top began to come up as she cruised up the paved driveway. "Most of the time, I'm here alone."

The driveway was lined with tall palm trees on both sides, and colorful lights illuminated the space. A three-car garage sat to the right of the house. She pressed another button, and the middle bay door rolled up. Baby Girl pulled inside, and Jaya was even more impressed. To her right was a yellow Lamborghini, and a 600 Series Mercedes-Benz sat to her left.

"Damn, girl, you living good," Jaya said with excitement.

Baby Girl switched off the engine, took a deep breath, and looked at Jaya. "It's all right. Sometimes things can look good as far as material shit, but if you ain't comfortable, it really don't mean shit."

"Basically, you're saying that everything that look good ain't good."

"Right," Baby Girl said, and pulled the latch on the door handle. "Come on," she told Jaya as she stepped out the car.

They went through the utility door into the kitchen. Jaya admired the stainless steel appliances and marble topped island and counter. Baby Girl went toward the family room and hit the light switch. Expensive furniture was everywhere; leather sofa and double stuffed chairs, thick wall-to-wall carpet, and the showstopper, a cherry wood long bar with a stained glass backdrop.

"Make yourself at home," Baby Girl said.

Jaya sat down in one of the stuffed leather chairs and was promptly swallowed up. The chair felt like a big hug, and she liked it.

Baby Girl went behind the bar. "I'm going to make some daiquiris," she announced.

"Cool, but what time are we gonna handle our business?"

Baby Girl pulled out a bottle of Hennessey and opened it. "I don't think we are going to handle any business this trip, Shonice. The Feds were at the club tonight, and I'm sure they were watching me. If they're watching me, they're watching you too.

That statement frightened Jaya a little. The first thing that came to mind was that Santonio would be pissed if she didn't come back with the dope. She frowned, not knowing what to say or do. One thing was certain, she wasn't about to get locked up if she didn't have to. She stood to her feet, and just as she was walking over to the bar where Baby Girl was standing, the phone rang.

Baby Girl hurried around from the back of the bar. She nearly ran to the couch where her bag was and pulled out her phone.

"Hello, Mister," she said.

The robotic voice that came from the other end said, "No more business, we on hold for everything." Then the line went dead.

Baby Girl ended the call and addressed Jaya. "Look, baby," she said. "I don't know how serious this situation is, but I will not be able to get you what you came for. I damn sho don't want to get you caught up in what we got going on down here. First things first, I'ma call you a cab. I want you to go back to your room, and from there, take your ass back to Georgia."

Jaya froze for a moment. She heard everything Baby Girl said loud and clear, but it was not what she needed to hear. This could not be a blank trip; she needed that cocaine. Her heart began to pound.

"So, ain't no way whatsoever that I can get at least five keys?"

Baby Girl shook her head as she gave the cab company her address and Jaya's destination. After arranging the cab, she walked over to Jaya, still holding her phone in her hand.

"I don't know how serious this matter is, but you need to do what I said, okay?" Baby Girl went back to the bar and poured herself a half glass of Hennessey and downed it immediately. "Come on, get you a drink before the cab gets here."

Jaya went over to the bar. She was definitely in need of a drink. Her nerves had unraveled to the point that her hands were shaking. The word Feds seemed to scream repeatedly in her head. Baby Girl had already poured her a double shot of Hennessey straight when she got to the bar. Jaya took a sip, and the heat from the beverage settled in her throat. She took two more deep gulps, and it was gone.

Baby Girl smiled at her. "Seems like you a solid bitch, from as far as I can tell."

"You can come to Atlanta and hang out with me. I don't have any female friends at all," Jaya said.

Baby Girl came from behind the bar and hugged Jaya. "If it's meant for us to meet again, then we will. I damn sho hate we can't handle this move according to plan."

"Everything happens for a reason, right?" Jaya responded.

A horn sounded outside.

Baby Girl's brow furrowed. "Damn, that was fast," she said. "Come on."

She led Jaya to the front door. When they reached the foyer, she paused and said, "If you happen to get questioned by anybody, just let them know you flew down to see your girlfriend. Now, what I need you to do is tell the cab driver that you are going straight to the airport. That way, you can double back and get your money. I think the cab driver is the Feds."

Jaya thanked Baby Girl, and after one more quick hug, she walked out to the cab. She got in the backseat of the cab and closed the door. Nervous, she studied the driver. He had sharp emerald green eyes, a low haircut, and a neatly trimmed mustache.

He flipped the meter and asked, "Where you going, ma'am?"

Jaya's face crumpled and she forced tears into her eyes. "I'm ..." she paused and wiped her eyes with the back of her hand, "going to the airport."

As the driver pulled off, he looked at her in the rearview mirror, and said, "I thought your call was for the Fontainebleau hotel."

Something wasn't right; Jaya could feel it. That last statement had set off several alarms. Her cell phone rang and she reached into her bag to retrieve it. When she saw that it was Santonio calling, she hit the power button, turning the phone completely off.

Jaya dropped the phone back into her bag and took a deep breath. "I'm going to the airport, sir," she said. "I flew all the way down here, just to find out that my girlfriend has been cheating on me after three years together."

The agent glanced at her again, not sure what to say. He definitely had not expected this development. This definitely changed their plans. For the next twenty minutes, he rode in silence, occasionally, checking on her through the rearview mirror. The subject was eerily still, just staring out the window into the darkness. His heart went out to her; she looked so troubled and sad. He was a new agent, and this was his first assignment. Empathy and compassion for criminals could get you killed in his line of work, so he shook those soft feelings off and drove a little faster. Within minutes, they pulled up to Miami International Airport. The meter read $48.97.

Jaya pulled a one hundred dollar bill out and handed it to the undercover agent. "Thank you," she said, staring into his eyes.

Their hands touched briefly, as he accepted the money. He looked away and busied himself with getting her change. When he turned around to hand her the change, she was already heading toward the front entrance of the airport with her bag slung over her shoulder. He watched her until she was out of his sight, and then he picked up his phone and dialed a number.

"The young lady is clean," he said to his superior when he answered. "She is leaving Miami."

Chapter 8

Jaya went straight to the ladies room when she entered the airport. Her nerves were shot to hell, and small beads of sweat had formed on her forehead. She checked under the doors of each stall to ensure that she was alone. Her heart raced as she went into the last stall, locked the door, and pulled her cell phone from her bag. Tears flowed down her face as she sat down on the toilet and powered her phone on. Her hands shook slightly as she dialed Santonio's number.

"Talk to me," he answered in a frigid tone.

"The Feds are all over your people down here," she said as she wiped her tears. "When you called, I was in a cab with an undercover, driving to the airport. I had to tell him to bring me here so I wouldn't lead them to the money."

"Where is the money?"

"At the hotel. I'm about to go get it and fly back home."

"Wait, wait … this what you do. Go get the money, then go back to the airport and wait for my call. I got another connect down there. Ain't no way in hell you coming back empty handed."

Jaya couldn't believe what she was hearing. Fresh tears streamed from her eyes as she listened silently to Santonio's instructions. Her heart ached because it was clear that he cared more about his cocaine than he did about her.

"All right," was all she said.

"Just calm down, baby, everything gonna be all right," he said in a soothing tone.

Jaya took a deep breath, rolled off a few sheets of tissue paper, and wiped her eyes before hanging up the phone. She collected herself and stood up, still wiping her eyes. "Get it together, girl," she told herself. "Since when do you let anything or anyone defeat you? All you do is win."

She walked out of the stall and went to the sink. After washing her hands, she splashed her face with cold water and stared at her reflection in the mirror. In that moment, she saw something different in her eyes, something cold, and something strange. An energetic feeling washed over her, and the nervousness disappeared. Jaya picked up her bag and placed it on her shoulder, raked her hair with her fingers, and left the bathroom.

The ticketing area was quiet. It was pretty late at night, and most of the airlines had departed their last flight for the night. Jaya decided to walk to the next terminal and find a cab. She did not want to use the same entrance, just in case the undercover agent was lurking.

When Jaya reached the north terminal and walked through the electronic glass doors, her nerves returned. Several cabs lined the curb, but after what she'd just experienced, each of them looked like the Feds to her. She squared her shoulders and found her stride. At the end of the block was an older Cuban looking guy leaning against his cab and smoking a Marlboro cigarette. A cloud of smoke lingered in front of his face.

Jaya stopped in front of him. "Are you working?"

He nodded and took another drag of his cigarette. Without saying a word, he thumped the cigarette to the ground and opened the rear door for Jaya. Once he was behind the wheel, he turned to Jaya and said, "Where you going?"

"Fontainebleau Hotel," was all she said.

———

Two hours later, Jaya was back at the airport, sitting in the ticketing area with the suitcase filled with money at her feet. She sipped her coffee and tapped her foot against the linoleum floor, trying desperately to stay awake. Her body was threatening to shut down. It was now 3:30 AM, and she had been awake for almost twenty-four hours. Tired did not begin to describe her current situation. She clutched her cell phone in her hand, anxiously awaiting the call from Santonio. He still hadn't called, and she was beginning to wonder if he'd forgotten about her. "Nah," she said to herself as she set her coffee down, "he didn't forget about his money."

Five minutes later, she gave up the fight and drifted off to sleep. In her dream, she was underwater in a wetsuit and fins, an oxygen tank on her back. Next to her was Santonio, she could see him smiling behind his facemask. She smiled back at him as they swam amongst the colorful fish, enjoying herself, enjoying life. Jaya had already made up her mind that she wanted to spend the rest of her life with him.

"Jaya," he called her name.

Her eyes flew open and she did a double take. She blinked a few times to make sure that she was not dreaming. Santonio was standing in front of her in jeans, a Polo blazer with a button down underneath, and a Louis Vuitton bag slung over his shoulder. Jaya couldn't believe her eyes; he'd come all the way down for her.

She stood up and wrapped her arms around his neck. "I'm so glad to see you," she said, with her face buried in his neck.

"I'm glad you all right, baby," he said and kissed her lips. "Let's get out of here," Santonio said as he picked up her bags.

After a quick visual scan of the area, Jaya pulled up next to him, and they walked side by side.

"Where we going?" she asked.

"To a hotel first, then we'll get some rest. I gotta come up with a plan.

Jaya listened closely, straining to catch every word as if she were eavesdropping. Whatever he said, she would agree with. As long as they were together, nothing else mattered.

––––––––

Jaya and Santonio had checked into the JW Marriott. The luxury hotel was like an escape from reality, but still located in the middle of the action. Santonio had stayed there often when he needed to be in the mix, but not on the scene.

Once they entered the spacious room with the glass balcony overlooking the ocean, all exhaustion was forgotten. In minutes, they were both naked. Jaya stood between Santonio's legs as he sucked on her breasts, going from nipple to nipple. Her head was thrown back, and her eyes were closed; she was enjoying the assault of his tongue and mouth on her body.

"Oooh, you got my pussy so wet," she said between moans, her hands rubbing all over his head.

He spun her around and laid her on the bed. She opened her legs immediately and invited him in. Santonio climbed on top of her, his slightly curved dick standing at attention. When he entered her, she got that feeling she craved. Her heart seemed to skip a beat, and butterflies invaded her stomach along with his manhood. Santonio went deep, pulled out a little and went deep again until Jaya was gasping, moaning, begging and grinding her pussy against him at the same time. When Jaya came, he came with her. Twenty minutes later, they came together again.

Finally, the two of them went to sleep and woke up, and hours later, they woke up to the setting sun. Jaya looked over at Santonio, who was lying on his back with his arm underneath his head, staring at the ceiling.

She rubbed the side of his face, and in a sleepy voice, she asked, "What's the matter?"

"Just stressing a little bit," he said, then added, "I got word about an hour ago that my people down here got snatched up by the Feds."

"What about Baby Girl, did they get her too?"

"I'm not sure who all they got, but when the Feds come you, nine times out of ten, they come for everybody."

Jaya slowly rubbed Santonio's face. She cared so much for him, and it made her sick to her stomach to see him restless and upset. Stretching her small hand across his chest, she kissed his cheek. "Stop stressing, baby, you don't have nothing to ever worry about."

That made him smile a little. His eyes went to Jaya and he pulled her on top of him. With his hands around her waist, he just held on to her. Jaya giggled as his stomach rumbled.

"Let me up, so I can order some room service," she said with a smile.

"Sounds like a plan to me."

She placed her lips on his. "I love you so damn much, Santonio. I wanna be with you forever."

"And you will."

Chapter 9

Back in Atlanta the next day, Santonio stood in his kitchen with an old man named Tommy. He was in his mid-fifties, tall and slender, with nappy grey hair. Santonio had him over for one reason, and that was to cook up his cocaine. When he'd cooked up the first kilo, and only 230 grams came back out of a thousand, he knew something was wrong.

The old man looked at Santonio and said, "Pimp, look like you bought a bad batch this time."

Santonio was already angry and pouring sweat, looking at the old man and then down at the dope. He couldn't believe it. "So, you mean to tell me that out of a whole fucking key, I only got two hundred and thirty grams back?"

The old man, Tommy's voice was deep and raspy. "Look like a nigga flexed you, pimp. Now, I don't know if the other nine is like that, but if I were you, I'd be on the phone with the niggas that sold you this shit.

Santonio took a long deep breath, his eyes shifting from the cocaine to the old man. "Cook up another one," he said angrily and walked into the living room.

He picked up his cellphone from the couch and dialed the guy in Miami's number. Santonio sat down on the sofa as he waited for his connect to answer. "I know this nigga ain't tried me like this," he said to himself.

There was no answer.

He called the number back, and once again, it rang and rang. The voicemail came on, and he left a message after the beep. "Aye brah, this ATL, hit me back at this number when you get this message. It's important."

Santonio hung up the phone and tossed it back on the couch, then went back to the kitchen where Tommy was tearing the duct tape and plastic from one of the kilos. He weighed out five hundred grams, two hundred fifty grams of baking soda, and mixed it up in a big brown Vision cookware pot. No more than twenty minutes later, they got the same results from the second kilo. Most of the cocaine had disappeared in the water, and by the time it dried, the five hundred grams had turned into ninety-seven.

It was obvious that Santonio had been had. Staring in disbelief, he could do nothing but shake his head in disgust. He went back into the living room and dialed the same number. This time, someone answered on the third ring.

"Yo."

Santonio got some life back in him when he heard a voice. "Hey, what's good, brah? Aye, the package was a defect. Shit ain't bouncing back right."

"All right," the guy said from the other end.

"All right, what?"

"Look, dawg, you sounding all aggressive and shit. What the fuck you gone do? Bring the dope back and come get your money back? Hell naw, you gone chalk that shit up as a loss, nigga."

Click!

Santonio sat frozen for a long moment, still holding the phone in his hand, and thinking, *I know I didn't just hear this nigga say, "Chalk it up as a loss."* He laughed half-heartedly to himself, just enough to make his chest rise and fall one solid time.

Tommy walked in from the kitchen, breaking Santonio from his thoughts. He looked up at him and said, "Ain't never been got like this." He was tired, drained, and looked as if all his life had left him.

"Two things you can do. Chalk it up and bounce back, or go down to Miami and kill the nigga that tried you."

As Santonio pondered Tommy's words, he heard a key turn in the front door. Jaya walked in smiling from ear to ear. She ran over to him and jumped in his lap.

"Baby, you ain't gonna believe this, she said happily.

"What is it?"

"I'm pregnant!"

Book 2
New York, New York

Chapter 10

Cleve was scheduled to go in to work at 7:00 AM, and he was already forty minutes late. That was nothing, because he was a compulsive liar and already had his story prepared for his manager. Heavy traffic was one of the best excuses to use in New York. A bomb threat on the subway was a good one to use also. Cleve thumped the butt of a Newport out the car window and raised it back up. He was dark-skinned heavyset and in his mid-thirties.

Smiling to himself, Cleve gripped the steering wheel and changed lanes. "Fuck it, yo," he said under his breath as he smoothly navigated his Q45 off the highway.

Small drops of rain began to fall as he pulled up to the loading dock of the electronics store where he worked. Cleve looked up at the sky and rubbed his full beard as the light rain sprinkled his windshield. He stepped out, dressed in a leather polo jacket, baggy jeans, and brown Timberland boots. The rain came down harder, popping against his jacket as he closed the door and went around to his trunk. He pulled out his umbrella and opened it, still facing the trunk, looking at nothing in particular. The rain had developed into a heavy pour, and he felt his nicotine urge coming back.

Behind him, he heard car tires rolling to a stop against the wet asphalt. A familiar voice called out, "Ole Cleve Banks."

Cleve didn't turn from his trunk. If someone was calling him by his government name like that, he figured something had to be wrong. He took a deep breath as two well-dressed federal agents pulled up on each side of him. Cleve looked from his left to his right; neither man seemed at all disturbed by the rain.

The agent on his right pushed a fat pink hand out to Cleve. "I'm Federal Agent Walsh," he said, his beady eyes directly on him. Walsh pointed to the other detective. "This is Federal Agent Long."

Cleve ignored Walsh's outstretched hand, but he did turn his head and examine the face of Agent Long. He had a strong chin and high cheekbones.

Agent Long nodded briefly at Cleve and said, "We need to ask you a few questions."

"Questions about what?"

"Several things," Walsh responded. "Maybe tax evasion, maybe counterfeit money. How about money laundering?"

Cleve held is composure then took another deep breath and ran his hand across his chubby face. "I'm already late for work, and ..."

"Sir, listen," Agent Long cut him off. "We're definitely aware of your criminal activity. We know about the Arabs, we know about the Russian connect. However, our interest is in the young lady, Joi Davis."

Cleve's eyes darted back and forth between both agents. His mind raced as he tried his best to keep his panic from showing.

"You're still on federal probation also, correct?"

Beads of sweat danced across Cleve's forehead. "Yo, so what you want?"

"Just a few questions."

Cleve got lost in his thoughts, wondering why in the hell they were asking about Joi. Did she do something? What the fuck? He shook his head in disgust, refusing to go back to prison for anybody. Stress flowed through him as he thought about his kids. He looked into Walsh's cold blue eyes. "How long is it gonna take?"

"An hour at the most."

Ten minutes later, they were riding through New York. The agents were in the front seat, and Cleve was in the back. Walsh handed Cleve a manila envelope with some 6x9 color photos inside. The first photo was of Joi leaning against the front of a glossy black Range Rover with another petite female, eating candy apples.

He flipped to the next photo, it was her again, this time she was walking with a foreign looking guy on the campus of New York University. Cleve recognized the Arab, but he didn't say anything. The third photo was of Joi again, this time she was sitting in a restaurant across from an older guy who Cleve didn't recognize. That was the last photo.

They were going over the Brooklyn Bridge when Walsh said, "We wanna know about this counterfeit money ring that she's running."

I don't really know her personally," Cleve answered.

"But you've been seen with her on several occasions," the agent said and handed Cleve another envelope.

Nervously, Cleve opened the envelope and removed more photos. The first one was him and Joi sitting next to each other on a bench in

Central Park feeding pigeons. The next photo was of Joi handing him a leather envelope bag. Damn! He remembered that day like it was yesterday. She'd given him twenty-five grand to make a run for her and her people two months ago.

"You still don't know her personally?" Walsh asked.

Cleve cut his eyes up at Walsh, stared at him for a moment without saying anything. He knew they had him dead to rights. Trying to buy some time, he flipped to the next photo. It was of him with four other people. Everyone was casually dressed and sitting around a table covered with champagne bottles, candles, and exotic food dishes. Joi was sitting next to him with her cell phone against her face. Cleve shook his head.

Agent Walsh said in a calm voice, "We know she is twenty-two years old, a student at NYU, and she cleans money for the Arabs through fake businesses and bank accounts. We also know that you're on her payroll as the muscle. Now let me hear your side of the story. Save yourself, Cleve."

"Fuck you mean, save myself?"

Agent Walsh turned back around and stared out the front windshield. He produced a small tape recorder, held it up, and without looking back, pressed the play button.

"Yo son, this little bitch, Joi, is doing too much. She's getting the big head, she's reckless with the counterfeit money. I hate bitches that think they're so smart, 'til they're stupid. I'm not going back to the Feds for this bitch."

The tape stopped and Walsh turned back around to face Cleve. "Now, let's try this again."

Chapter 11

The rain had stopped by the time they brought Cleve back. When the Crown Victoria pulled up in the rear parking lot where his Q45 was still parked, he scanned the area to see if anyone was around that he knew or who even knew him. Everything looked good and clean, except for an older bag lady who was pushing a buggy and digging in the green dumpster. Cleve sat back for a moment and thought about everything he'd said in the last hour. He felt guilty as hell inside; he'd actually spilled his guts, even giving up information about Joi's little brother and the chop shop ring. They didn't even ask for that.

Walsh handed Cleve his card with his direct phone number on it. "I expect to be hearing from you in no less than forty-eight hours."

Cleve pushed the card down in his front pocket, shook both of their hands and stepped out. The New York wind was whipping after the rain. He closed the door, bent down, and laced up his boots as the Feds pulled off.

The car stopped, backed up, and the passenger side window came down. Federal Agent Walsh looked at the Q45, examining it closely. Then he said to Cleve, "What about your car?"

Cleve stood up and looked at him. "What about it?"

"Is it stolen? Did you get it from the chop shop as well?"

Cleve just stood there staring at them until they laughed and pulled off. He was supposed to head into work. However, he now felt different. The last hour had changed things for him. He was in a situation where he wasn't trying to go out bad, but either way, it was all bad. He just tried to convince himself that it wasn't.

———————

The following day, Joi was walking down the corridor of the downtown Manhattan building she lived in. She lived in a high-rise apartment building with a beautiful lobby that was laced with antique furniture that looked like it came from a castle in England, along with marble floors and brass elevators. Her apartment was on the twelfth floor, a nice, quiet spot. All the doors were painted white and trimmed with gold. Joi was a flashy dresser and she loved to stand out. Today's attention grabber was her tight denim jeans, white leather boots, and white leather waist length jacket.

Joi could hear the phone ringing inside her apartment as she walked up to the door. Moving quickly, she slid her key into the lock and twisted the door handle. After stepping in the foyer and closing the door, she raced into the living room and stopped short when she spotted her brother relaxing on the L-shaped suede sofa. The cordless phone was next to him, and he had a rolled blunt pressed between his fingers.

The phone stopped ringing, and he looked up at Joi with red, nearly closed eyes. He was big; muscular, six foot one and handsome. At only twenty-one years old, they called him Big Bank Hank in the streets.

Joi went straight to him, shoved his head, snatched his do-rag off and threw it in his face. "Stupid, you're sitting here just letting the phone ring and won't answer it!"

Big Bank Hank blew a stream of smoke from his mouth while looking directly at her. "Calm down, sis." His tone was smooth and relaxed. He had a nonchalant personality, always speaking as if everything was all right. "It wasn't nobody but Lisa. She's been blowing me up all day, vexing me out about she's pregnant." He pulled on the blunt again.

Joi's eyes were trained on him now. He had her undivided attention. "Do you think it's your seed?" she asked him.

"Hell no." He exhaled the smoke. "Shorty got a nigga. She on some confused shit. Bitch see a nigga getting' a lil cake, and she wanna make me her baby daddy. Not today, and damn sure not tomorrow."

Joi put her hands on her waist, shaking her head at him in disbelief. "Just like a nigga," she said. "Boy, you'll make Mom and Pop roll over in their graves." Then, she reached for the blunt.

He flashed a half grin, examining his sister from top to bottom. "One day you smoke, then you don't," he said, but he gave her the blunt anyway.

The phone rang again just as Big Bank Hank stood up. He picked it up and ended the call without saying a word. "Rent thirty-five hundred a month in this bitch," he said to Joi.

Joi sat down, pulled on the blunt, holding it between her French tips. When she blew the smoke from her mouth, she rolled her eyes at him. "And it's probably gonna get higher, nigga. So what you saying?"

Big Bank Hank smiled at his sister. "Damn, girl, you thank about money more than me."

Before she could respond, the phone rang again. He was about to answer it, but Joi snatched the phone up first with her free hand and handed him the blunt with the other one. She put her finger up to her mouth. "Hello," she said as she stood up, holding the phone in the crook of her neck.

She came out of her jacket, just as the female on the other end said, "Who is this?" in an aggressive tone.

Joi's whole demeanor changed. "What the fuck you mean, 'who is this?' Who is this?"

Click!

Joi's eyebrows rose, she was quick-tempered and far beyond arrogant. She could do nothing but look at the phone and press her thin lips together. Joi had pretty hazel eyes and a smooth, thin face. She was 5'4", a yellow bone, with hair like an Indian. She carried herself very well around the city of New York. When she was fifteen years old and her brother was fourteen, both her parents were killed in a car accident. The siblings were separated for nearly eighteen months when they went to separate homes. Joi was adopted by a Dominican family who put her in a private school where she became an A-plus student, graduated with honors, and then went to NYU. However, Joi had a bad side to her, she plugged in with some Brooklyn Arabs a couple years ago, where she learned the income tax game. She was good at it, stealing names and filing taxes by creating businesses that did not exist. That opened up other hustles for her, like getting plugged in with a team of females with A-1 looking counterfeit money.

Now, here she was, doing exceptionally well for herself. She'd reunited with her brother, and although he was doing his own things in the streets, no money or anything else would ever come between them.

Joi tossed the phone on the couch and looked at her brother. "I swear, I don't know what kind of hood bitches you be fucking with."

Big Bank Hank looked her in the eyes, pulled on the blunt again, and then French rolled the smoke before he passed Joi the blunt. She put it between her lips, leaned down, and took her shoes off as the phone rang again.

Joi smiled. Her teeth were white and even. She looked at her brother and just shook her head at him. "Yes?" she said into the phone once again.

"What up, Ma?" a deep voice said from the other end. It was Cleve.

"Hey, Papi," she shot back. Her eyes rolled a little as she looked toward her brother and he caught the hint that the call was for her.

Big Bank Hank relaxed a bit, knowing that it wasn't Lisa again. He walked over to the floor to ceiling windows and parted the drapes a bit to indulge in the spectacular view of the New York skyline before he headed toward his room.

Joi watched him disappear around the corner as Cleve said, "Look, Ma, I don't wanna talk over the phone, but I need to see you. It's very important."

Joi immediately went on the defense. "Come see me," was all she said before hanging up the phone.

Damn, she thought. Her mind raced faster. She thought about her stash; she had money put up in bank accounts, but nothing was hidden. Still holding the phone in her hand, she redialed the number and waited for an answer.

"Yo." Cleve said.

"Papi, I don't feel right."

"What's wrong?"

"I don't know, my gut is telling me that something isn't right." She shook her head. "Give me a couple days, and I'll contact you, okay?"

"No, we need to meet up today, Joi."

Without another word, Joi ended the call. She was high and paranoid, but her gut was telling her right. After closing the drapes back, she walked to Hank's bedroom and knocked briefly before going in.

Big Bank Hank was curling a fifty pound dumbbell in the mirror with his left arm, and smoking the blunt with his right

Joi sat on the bed behind him. "Listen, if anything ever happens to me, I want you to handle Cleve for me."

He looked at her in the mirror at first, but when her words finally registered, he turned around and faced her. "What's wrong?"

Without responding, she got up and went to the window. As she stared down at the busy congested traffic of Manhattan, she heard her brother burst out laughing, and turned around to look at him.

"Yooo, you trippin'. I told you this isn't no regular smoke.

Joi laughed shortly and then her smile faced. "I want Cleve handled, dead.

And she meant it.

Chapter 12

Night was coming quickly. Cleve parked his Q45 in the parking deck in lower Manhattan's Soho/Tribeca area. The cool New York air whipped through his jacket as he stepped out of the car. He zipped his jacket and pulled up his collar as he headed toward a ramp that led him to a glass door. After Cleve punched in a security code on the wall, the lock clicked and he went through the door. An elevator was to his left. Cleve had his own key, which he slipped into the lock. The doors to the elevator opened and Cleve looked both ways before stepping in.

He got off on the eighth floor. There was a white couple walking side by side and holding hands just ahead of him. He walked a few more feet and stopped in front of an apartment door on his right. He knocked lightly. One ... Two ... Three ... One, two. It was a code. He didn't hear anything on the other side of the door, and then it came open. Cleve stared into the eyes of a dark-skinned African man with uncombed nappy hair. He was in khaki pants, no shirt, with a leather gun holster on his shoulders and a short AK assault rifle in his hand, resting on the side of his leg. He stared at Cleve for a moment, then he moved to the side and allowed him to step in. The African stuck his head out the door and scanned the hallway. It was clear, so he closed the door.

The African led Cleve further into the living room, it was dimly lit, decorated in glossy oak wood and black lacquer. There was a three-piece black leather sofa set surrounding a low coffee table. In the leather chair sat an older light skinned man with hazel eyes, smoking a Cuban cigar. He was dressed in a two-piece pajama set. A huge Cuban link chain was around his neck, and he motioned his head for Cleve to have a seat.

He sat down across from him and said, "I believe this chick, Joi, is snitching."

The man puffed his cigar and a cloud of smoke curled up around his face. He didn't respond, he just sat there watching Cleve, staring in his eyes. Then he asked, "Where are these allegations coming from?"

Cleve pushed his body up a little bit and pulled out a Newport from his front pocket along with a lighter. He lit a cigarette and pulled from it. The Feds pushed up on me today when I was going to work, and everything they had to say, Joi Davis name came up in it. Recordings, pictures and everything. I tried to call her to let her know that we needed to speak, but she's avoiding me. I think she knows what's up."

The old man sat in silence for a moment, a line of wrinkles formed on his forehead as he shook his head from side to side. He leaned up and set the burning cigar in the ashtray, then he looked up at the African bodyguard. "Send for Joi."

"No, let me go," Cleve said quickly and jumped up.

The old man studied Cleve for a moment. His eyes were telling a lie, and that wasn't good. "Let me call her first."

———

When Joi's doorbell rang, she was relaxing in her oval shaped tub with scented candles all around her. Mary J. Blige was bumping as she sipped wine from a glass. Covered in suds, she pushed herself up and out of the water. She wrapped in a robe and walked toward the front door. A half grin appeared across her face as she looked through the peephole.

"What the fuck you want, Shi?" She yelled through the door.

"I'm looking for your brother, I don't want you," he responded from the other side.

Joi pulled her robe tighter, then she unlocked the door. She looked up at Shi. He was way taller than she was, at least six foot three, and dressed in the normal gear, baggy jeans, Timbs, and an Avirex leather jacket. Shi was Big Bank Hank's right hand man, he was three years younger than Joi, but he was definitely handsome.

"Damn, you look sexy as fuck when you're high," he said to Joi.

Joi couldn't help the blush that spread across her cheeks as she pushed his chest and sucked her teeth. "Boy, you better get your life right."

Shi went back a couple steps from her shove, but he came right back at her. "No, shorty, I'm for real. You make a young, rich thug like myself want to change his life." He grabbed both of her hands and she didn't resist.

She wrinkled her nose. "You're still too young, honey." Then she pulled her hands away from him, turned and headed for her bedroom. She looked back at him, giving him a seductive glance.

He stood there smiling with his arms folded. "All right, lil mama, you gonna keep bullshittin' and fuck around and miss your blessing. When I sign this record deal with Jay-Z, you'll be all over my dick."

Joi heard him talking shit, but she kept it moving and didn't even respond. She eased back into her room and removed her robe. Mary J was still playing on low, just like she left it. Her phone lay on her bed turned off completely. She didn't want any calls, and neither did her brother. In the bathroom, she removed her robe, stepped back in the tub and returned to her relaxed mode. In the back of her mind, she knew that something wasn't right, but she didn't want to deal with just yet. She tilted her head back with her eyes closed and allowed the soothing sound of Mary J. Blige to relax her.

———

Big Bank Hank and Shi were in Hank's room. Shi leaned against the cherry wood dresser with a Glock 19 in his hand. He examined it carefully, popping the clip out; it was full. Then, he looked over at Hank. He was sitting on the bed loading bullets into an AK banana clip.

"Who loaded this clip, yo?" Shi asked.

Hank looked up at him. "For extra precaution, take 'em out and wipe them 'em down." He paused; his eyes were cold. "We going to pay this nigga, Cleve, a visit before he makes the wrong move."

"Say no more, son."

It took Shi about five more minutes to remove the shells from the clip and load them back in, using a handkerchief. When he was done, he picked up the remote and hit the power button on the TV.

"Come on and get your ass beat in NBA Live one time."

Hank was engrossed in checking the AK 47, his hands covered by gloves. "My mind is on some other shit right now," Hank said without looking up.

Shi turned on the game. "Yo, don't stress yourself, son. That shit is gonna get handled, and that's my word."

Big Bank Hank removed the gloves from his hands and relit the blunt that was in the ashtray. He pulled on it, then said, "Lisa sayin' I got her pregnant, son."

"And."

"And what?" Hank asked with a frown.

"And one, nigga." Shi laughed and turned on the game.

Big Bank Hank met Shi's eyes. "Fuck are you talking about, And one?"

Shi couldn't help but to laugh again as the blunt was passed back and forth. "You drove to the rim, scored, but it was a foul on the play, son."

Hank laughed a little then picked up the other PlayStation remote, with the burning blunt still pressed between his lips. He eased the AK under the bed.

Just then, they heard Joi yell from her room, "Shi, come here for a minute."

Shi flipped his head toward Hank, hoping that he didn't have a problem with his sister calling him, but Hank seemed unbothered.

"I'll be right back," Shi said.

Shi stepped inside Joi's room. It was cozy, spacious, and smelled like peaches. He paused when he saw her sprawled across her Queen sized bed, looking exotic against the black satin sheets. She was on her stomach. Her lower body was covered, but he could easily see her hips and ass under the sheet.

Joi looked back at him; her eyes had that 'come fuck me' look. In a gentle tone, she said, "Can you lotion me down, please?"

Shi couldn't believe his ears or his luck. His heart beat erratically and he felt himself growing harder with each passing second. Telling himself to relax and be easy, he closed the door and went to the bed. Joi was laying with her arms folded underneath her head as Shi sat on the bed next to her.

"Get that oil right there on the nightstand," Joi said. "And start with my back." Her eyes were closed and her head was turned in the opposite direction from where Shi sat.

Shi picked up the small bottle of oil and poured it into the groove of Joi's back. She quivered under Shi's touch. His strong hands and long fingers massaged her back, shoulders, and neck. As she relaxed, her ass arched in the air.

"Rub my ass," she whispered, still never looking at him.

When he moved the sheet from her ass, she felt the cool air kiss her posterior. Shi had never seen a prettier ass and shaved vagina than hers. She was gorgeous from head to toe. When he moved his finger down the slit of her ass crack and touched her pussy, she moved back toward him.

"I didn't say touch my pussy, but it feels good," Joi murmured.

With that being said, Shi kicked off his boots one at a time, and then he stood up. When Joi looked back at him, he was taking his pants off and pulling a condom from his back pocket at the same time. He ripped the condom package open with his teeth while stepping out of his pants.

Joi smiled and twisted her body in preparation for what he had to offer. Shi pulled his boxers down, and Joi saw that he was working with something. She was ready. Impatiently, she waited as Shi laced his dick with the condom, slowly rolling it on as he pulled his shirt over his head and tossed it to the floor.

He climbed up on the bed and pulled Joi up by her waist. Her ass was spread, pretty, round and glossy. Shi poured some of the oil down the crack of Joi's ass and then set the bottle down. He massaged her ass cheeks until he felt her body relax again, and then he gently guided his dick inside her. She was tight, and the warmth of her pussy felt so good to him, that all he could do was close his eyes and whisper, "Damn."

Joi looked back at him, her tiny hands turning into fists as she gripped the sheets and threw her ass back. "Ohh shit," she moaned and moved in a rhythm that matched his thrusts.

Shi was desperately trying to control himself, thinking about walking to the top of the Statue of Liberty when he was younger just so he wouldn't cum too fast. Joi was giving it to him, winding her hips and grinding.

Don't move, Ma," he said and closed his eyes, praying to last a little bit longer, at least until she came one time.

"Go ahead and beat it, Papi. You asked for this pussy, now get it." Her tone was low, soft and demanding.

Don't talk to me! Fuck she talking for? He said to himself. He felt it coming from his chest, down through his stomach; he was about to cum. He started to beat it hard. Sweat beads formed on his forehead. "Shit," he growled. "Damn! I'm about to cum."

Joi kept ramming her ass cheeks against his pelvis, but she knew he wasn't prepared. She could feel him going soft inside of her, and fixed him with the most disappointed look he'd ever seen on a woman. "Your dick game is zero. You couldn't even last ten minutes."

"I couldn't help it," Shi said as he pulled his limp dick and full condom out. He looked down at himself and shook his head. "Just give me five minutes, Joi, and let me get myself together."

She frowned, twisted her mouth in one corner, and tumbled over on her back while he stood there baffled and embarrassed. "Come on, nigga."

She crooked her finger and spread her legs. "Come eat my pussy. You got me started, and you're gonna finish."

Joi started rubbing her clit, making her fingers disappear between her pussy lips.

Shi stood there, staring at her for a moment, watching her play with herself, and then he didn't think any longer. He carefully got down between her legs and began to kiss her pussy lips. Joi moved her hand, allowing him full access. He clearly did not know what he was doing, but it didn't feel bad. After a few minutes, she made him stop.

"Get up," Joi said, pushing his head away.

Shi raised his head and looked into her eyes. "What's the matter?" he asked while wiping his mouth.

"See you later, Shi."

Joi tried her best to speak warmly, but he'd turned her off. She lifted her body, pulled the satin sheet up and turned over on her side. She didn't say another word to him.

Shi was so messed up in his head that he just got himself together and left quietly.

Joi lay on her bed, staring at the ceiling. Her mind was spinning in several directions. She had wanted to fuck in order to ease mind and to relieve some stress, but it didn't work out like that. Things rarely go as planned. Joi touched herself; she was wet and horny. In an instant, her mind flashed back to several months ago.

On that particular night, it was hot, even for New York. The sticky kind of hot that made everyone irritable, but the heat didn't faze Joi at all. She and her homegirl, Asia, stepped out of the Cotton Club, both of them dressed in designer short shorts, halter-tops, and low heels. With their hair, nails and toes all done, they just knew that they were ready to be the next video vixen. The traffic was thick, bumper to bumper up and down Broadway near 125th St. There were big body Benzes, 600 V12s, limousines, Hummers, Lexus, Jaguar, you name it. The expensive sound systems in some of the cars had the groupies dancing and bobbing their heads. The beat from the Hummer was the loudest.

Joi sucked on a red Blow Pop as she and Asia walked across Broadway. Out of nowhere, a clean olive green Q45 cut them off. Joi paused and her eyebrows rose as she tried to see through the tinted windows.

The driver side window lowered, and the fruity smell of marijuana seeped out of the car. Joi took her Blow Pop from her mouth slowly, allowing her lips to seductively pop around it. The driver was dark and handsome, and when his hand came out the window, he was holding a gold bottle of Cristal champagne, unsealed.

"It's the Brooklyn way, ma," he said to Joi.

"Thank you, papi." She took the bottle, then leaned down and kissed him on the cheek. He wore his beard like Gerald Levert and had a big sparkling diamond in his left earlobe.

A familiar voice from the passenger seat caught her attention. "Papi, papi, papi ... Is that all you can say?"

Joi eased the Blow Pop into her mouth, twirled it around, and took it out, then she looked over at the passenger seat. "I know that's not Cleve," she said, smiling.

Asia, who recognized the voice as well, looked into the car and her whole demeanor changed. She frowned at him and rolled her eyes. Then she looked at Joi. "Give me the keys, I'll be in the truck."

Cleve opened his door and swung his frame out of the car, holding a New York Yankee fitted cap in one hand and his own personal chilled bottle of Cristal in the other. "C'mon, Asia, are you serious right now? You can't be still upset." His arms were spread out as if he were waiting for a hug as he walked around the car toward Asia.

The man in the driver seat was named Tyrone, but they called him Ty. He took his eyes off Joi and allowed his gaze to travel down the block to where Cleve had walked off with Asia. "What did son do to little shorty?"

Joi watched them for a moment, then she sucked on her Blow Pop and shrugged. "I'm not sure," she said.

"Let me pull over," Ty said and moved the Q45 to the curb and turned his hazard lights on. He put the car in park, and stepped out, holding two champagne glasses in his hand, and set them on the hood of the car.

Joi watched him. He was tall and slim, and her mind instantly pondered what size dick he had. *Control yourself,* she said silently as she peeled the gold foil from the bottle.

A few yards away, Asia and Cleve were cuddled up and talking. Cleve yelled, "Yo, Joi, that's my man, Ty. Talk to him."

Ty frowned and looked up the block toward Cleve, who had started walking back toward them, along with Asia.

"Damn! Y'all made up quick," Joi said.

Asia smiled. Cleve had his arm around her neck, and then he turned up the bottle of champagne. Some spilled and ran down the side of his face.

Ty said to him, "Son, you're drunk. Slow down."

Cleve looked at Ty through barely open eyes, and then said to Joi, "This my man right here, real official nigga, just came home from up state ..."

Ty took the bottle of champagne from Joi and pulled her up to him. He palmed her ass while looking at Cleve. "She cool people. We've already met, son, just relax."

A little over an hour later, Ty and Joi were pulling into the driveway of Asia's parents in Ty's Q45 behind Joi's Range Rover. Ty killed the lights. The Long Island neighborhood was nice and quiet. Ty and Joi had been passing a thin blunt back and forth, and she was feeling nice, like she was floating on a cloud. She was no stranger to smoking, but this was a different feeling.

Ty wasn't about to tell her that she was smoking Angel Dust. He flipped on the interior light and looked over at Joi. She looked so good against the soft leather seats. "You all right, Ma?" he asked in a low whisper as he reached over and pushed a few strands of hair from her face.

Joi kept her eyes closed as a smile played on her lips. "Yeah, I'm good, papi. My mouth a little dry," she said and sighed.

Ty took advantage of that and leaned over toward her. He licked the side of her neck and she tensed slightly. Not enough to make him stop, though.

"I like that," Joi murmured then took his hand and pulled it down between her legs.

Joi was hot and moist. She spread her legs and he worked his finger in her shorts and into her panties. Ty felt how wet her pussy was and got more excited than she was. Joi started rubbing on her own breasts, pushing one out of her halter and playing with her nipples. She began to wind her body against his fingers in small circles.

"You about to make me cum."

"That's what I wanna do," he responded.

He nibbled on her earlobe and dug deeper into her pussy. Then, as soon as she said, "Suck my titties," a light tap sounded against the window.

The noise made her jump. She looked to her right, and so did Ty, but neither of them saw anyone. Ty flipped off the interior light so he could see outside into the night. Just then, three bullets came through the driver side window, all three of them hitting Ty in his chest as glass shattered and exploded.

Joi couldn't believe it. She covered her mouth and ducked down on the floor as the gloved hand came in through the shattered driver side window. Joi saw the whites of the man's eyes behind the mask as he placed the barrel of the Ruger to Ty's head and squeezed the trigger.

———————

Joi shook her head at the memory. She hoped that Cleve hadn't put her name in anything related to the murder. As she pondered the situation, there was a loud knock at the door.

She hopped up and covered herself before saying, "Come in."

Her brother peeped his head inside. "I'm out, and I'll be out of town after I handle that business. Maybe Atlantic City, I'll let you know."

Joi studied him for a moment. "Be careful, ok," was all she said.

Hank nodded then closed the door.

Joi got up and went into the bathroom to pee. Sitting on the toilet, she thought long and hard. Something wasn't right, and she could feel it in her bones.

Chapter 13

Jaya's mother and stepfather owned a huge five-bedroom estate in Alpharetta, Georgia inside a gated community. In the high-ceilinged family room, Jaya sat on the leather double stuffed loveseat with her legs kicked up. Her shoes were off, and she was snacking on a bowl of chilled fruit. Karen, Jaya's mother, sat across from Jaya holding a glass of Welch's White Grape Juice and staring at her daughter.

"So, you're pregnant by a man that I've never met," Karen stated.

"I'm pregnant by a man that I am in love with, who is in love with me."

Karen sat quietly for a moment, sipping her grape juice. She was in her late forties, with a petite toned frame and smooth chocolate skin, thanks to yoga three times a week. An engineer at CNN, Jaya's mother, had a fearless look about herself, and she intimidated most men and women. She chose her words carefully, knowing that regardless of what she said, she probably wouldn't get through to her stubborn daughter.

The apple didn't fall far from the tree, and Karen knew that there was no reasoning with a fool in love.

"Are you gonna finish school, Jaya?"

"Of course, Mom, you're asking questions that are not even relevant right now." She paused, tossed a piece of melon into her mouth and sat up. "He asked me to marry him, Mom." She held her hand out and showed Karen a sparkling two-carat diamond ring.

Karen cut her eyes at the ring, not impressed at all. When her eyes went back to Jaya, she asked, "When do I get to meet him, Jaya?"

"When I come back from New York in a couple of days, we've arranged for me, you and him to go out to dinner. He's really cool, Mom, and trust me, I've told him about you." Jaya put her shoes on then stood up and walked over to her mother.

Karen stood up and put her arms around her daughter. She whispered, "Whatever you're doing, baby, please be careful, okay?" She squeezed Jaya tighter and they held onto each other for nearly three minutes.

Jaya felt a tear fall from her eye. "I love you, Mom, and I'll be careful, okay?"

She separated from her mother and left the house. It was mid-afternoon, and Jaya had to meet Santonio at her townhouse. She jumped in her car and dialed Santonio's number right away.

Santonio answered as she was pulling out of the long driveway. "Hey baby," he said.

"Hey, boo, I'm leaving my parents' house now."

"What you tell them?"

"Everything, that I'm pregnant and we're getting married."

"Your dad was there too?"

"My stepdad. No, he wasn't there, but he'll know. I told my mother I was going to New York, and when I come back, we are all going out to dinner."

"We definitely gonna make that happen. Your flight leaves in two hours, so meet me at your spot. Love you."

"Love you too, baby. I'm on the way."

———

Jaya and Santonio had met at her place and she'd changed clothes and parked her car. Now, they were riding together on 285. She stared into space, with a million and one things racing through her mind. Her mother's voice seemed to echo through her thoughts. Karen wanted her to finish school, and she wanted it for herself as well. On the other hand, she had a promising future with a man that she loved so damned much, that she could feel it creeping through her veins.

Santonio's phone rang, snapping Jaya out of her daydream. She looked over at him as he answered it.

"Yeah?" he said into the phone. His head and eyes were pointed straight forward, watching the traffic.

"So that's how you gonna respond to me, Santonio? After everything we've been through?" his girlfriend said.

Santonio took a deep breath. He tried to keep it calm, but she had him fire hot. "Look, we ain't got nothin' else in common. I'm with my fiancée right now, riding off into the sunset. You wanna speak to her?"

There was silence on the phone, and then the line went dead. Santonio frowned and pressed the end button.

Jaya stared at him. She couldn't believe what she'd just heard. Somewhere inside of her, she wanted to be angry, but on the other hand, she knew she couldn't be. Turning her gaze away from him, she swallowed hard and looked out the window.

The car was silent for the next few minutes as they drove. Santonio turned on the radio then immediately turned it back off. "All I want is for us to be all right, Jaya."

"When she turned and looked at him, there were tears in her eyes. She wiped them with the back of her hand. "Me too," she said, then added, "After this trip—"

Santonio cut her off. "This is your last trip, Jaya." He reached over and put his hand on her stomach. "We got a baby to raise. What we ain't got after this trip, we just ain't got, and that's a promise."

Jaya's tears turned to joy. She smiled at him and said, "If it's a boy, I want to name him Santonio, Jr."

Santonio smiled and nodded. "And if it's a girl, I want to name her Jaya."

For the next ten minutes, they talked about baby stuff, houses and high credit scores. Instead of pulling up to the curb at the airport, Santonio parked in the garage so he could spend a few extra moments with Jaya without police harassment. Jaya expelled a long breath and looked at Santonio then leaned toward him. He met her with a kiss, carefully sucking on her tongue. He held her face between his hands. Do you realize how much I love you?" he asked between kisses.

Kaya nodded and smiled. She pulled away from him and got herself together. As she fixed her makeup in the mirror, Santonio gave her instructions.

"Quick play by play. You're going to see my Dominican people. We're only coppin' four bricks this time, at sixteen five a piece. That means you'll be giving him sixty grand." He pointed to the glove compartment. "Grab that envelope out of there."

She opened the glove compartment and pulled out an envelope. "It's two grand in there, you already know the routine."

Both of them stepped out the car into the busy, noisy airport atmosphere. Jaya slung the tote bag over her shoulder and Santonio opened the rear door on his side and pulled out her leather wheeled carry-on suitcase. He walked around to where Jaya stood, and kissed her softly on her lips. "You got your Shanice Brooks license and everything?" Jaya nodded yes and he put the suitcase handle in her hand and kissed her cheek. "Call me as soon as you land, okay?"

Her eyes turned sad again, but she held her emotions with a smile. "Love you, boo."

"And you know I love you too," he said, then he turned and went back to the driver side of the car.

Jaya turned and headed toward the terminal entrance. When she got inside the airport, she got in line to print her boarding pass at one of the American Airlines kiosks. In her rush to make it to the airport on time, she had forgotten to print it at home. The airport was crowded with families and business people. As she waited behind two other travelers, her eyes swept the departures area. A little girl, maybe three years old, ran around in circles laughing. She looked so happy when the petite woman that Jaya assumed was her mother, snatched her up and kissed her. She carried the little girl while the man with them gathered their several pieces of Samsonite luggage. Jaya watched them and imagined a similar scene with her, Santonio and their baby.

"Ma'am, that kiosk is open over there," a male voice said, breaking into her daydream.

"Thank you," Jaya said and smiled at the man in line behind her.

Jaya walked up to the kiosk and printed her boarding pass. As she made her way through the security checkpoint, she thought about

Santonio's promise that this would be her last trip. She really hoped he kept his promise; the stakes were so much higher now that she was pregnant, and she didn't want to do anything to jeopardize their child.

Jaya had twenty minutes to spare before her flight would begin boarding, so she stopped at the Atlanta News and Gifts shop near her gate. She spotted a Robb Report magazine with a bright red Lamborghini on the cover and picked it up. After flipping through a couple of pages, she grabbed a bottle of water and took it along with the magazine to the checkout counter.

Twenty minutes later, she was stashing her bags in the overhead compartment before she took her window seat in first class. A few minutes later, a middle-aged white man in a suit and wire-framed glasses sat next to her. He gave her a warm smile, put his headphones on, and pulled out his Wall Street Journal.

A tall blonde flight attendant approached them. ""Ma'am is there anything that I can get you?" she asked.

"Sprite, please," Jaya answered.

"Would you like a pillow also?"

"Yes, thank you."

The flight attendant asked Jaya's seatmate if he wanted anything, but he just shook his head no, without looking up from his newspaper.

Jaya made herself comfortable and pulled out her magazine as the rest of the passengers boarded the plane. Moments later, as the plane took off, she felt her eyelids getting heavy. She was mentally exhausted. The flight attendant came back with her drink and pillow. As she sipped her drink, her mind traveled back in time.

She was five years old, and her mother was sitting in front of the computer with her reading glasses on. Jaya had on her nightgown and was holding her teddy bear by the arm.

"Mommy, is Daddy gone to heaven like my goldfish and Fluffy?"

"Yes, Jaya," her mother answered sadly.

"Well, Fluffy got hit by a car, and the goldfish got sick, so what happened to my daddy?"

Her mother turned away from the computer with tears in her eyes. She pulled Jaya to her and they cried together.

"I just want my daddy back, Mommy," little Jaya said between tears. "I don't want him to go to heaven. I want him here. Please bring him back, Mommy," she sobbed.

Karen wiped her eyes as she rocked her child. "Shh, it's going to be all right, baby. Shh…"

"Ma'am, are you all right?" the man sitting next to Jaya asked as he touched her arm.

Startled, Jaya opened her eyes and turned toward the man. She didn't realize that she had been crying until she noticed the tissue that he held out to her. She took the tissue and wiped her eyes. "Thank you, yes, I'm fine."

Jaya opened her magazine. On the first page was a Tiffany ad featuring a platinum and diamond wedding band. It was a beautiful piece of jewelry, but she felt that the price was outrageous.

"Thirty-five thousand dollars! Now they know that's too much," she blurted out and showed the page to the man in the next seat.

He looked at the ad and then up at her. "Well, you know what they say … If you have to question the price of anything, then you can't afford it.

Jaya just stared at him and said to herself, *Bastard.*

Chapter 14

It was already dark when Jaya stepped out into the chilly New York weather. The wind sliced through her jacket as she pulled her rolling suitcase behind her and adjusted the strap on her handbag. She approached the first cab she saw and got into the back seat. Jaya closed the door quickly, grateful to be out of the cold.

Before she could even get settled into the seat, the cab driver looked at her in the rearview mirror and rudely said, "Where to, lady?"

"The Marriott," she responded.

The driver was a middle-aged white man with a missing front tooth and a five o'clock shadow. "C'mon, lady, you're in New York City. It's a hundred Marriotts."

"Well, if you would've let me finish, I could've been more specific. Please take me to the Marriott East Side in Manhattan," she said in a tone that matched his rudeness.

Damn, is everybody rude up here? Jaya said to herself, thinking back to the man on the airplane. She just shook her head as the driver started the meter at four dollars and quickly pulled out into traffic. This was Jaya's first time in New York, and she was definitely excited and in tourist mode.

"Where is the Statue of Liberty?" she asked.

"You didn't see it as you flew into LaGuardia?"

Jaya turned up her nose and stared coldly at the back of the driver's head. He was so damned rude. She had an overwhelming urge to pop him right in his big ass bald spot. Instead, she focused her attention out of the window at the New York skyline as they drove into the city. For twenty minutes, they rode with country music playing through busted speakers. It nearly drove her crazy.

Finally, the raggedy cab pulled up in front of the Marriott. "Here you go, lady," the cantankerous cabbie announced.

Jaya laughed lightly, handed him two twenty dollar bills and snatched both of her bags. A handsome doorman opened the door, and she got out of the cab, not bothering to wait for change. The only thing she wanted was to get the hell away from him as quickly as possible.

"Welcome to the Marriott," he said. "Checking in?"

"Yes."

"Excellent. The front desk is right through those doors. Would you like your bags brought to your room?"

"Thanks, but I'm all right," Jaya said with a smile. She wasn't about to let her money leave her eyesight.

When she stepped into the lobby, the first thing that caught her eyes was the apricot colored marble floor and matching countertop. *I want this exact color for my house,* she thought as she approached the counter.

"Welcome to the Marriott, how may I help you this evening, ma'am," a young Hispanic male greeted her.

"Good evening, I have a reservation."

"What is your last name?"

"Brooks."

"Yes, I see your reservation. A king suite for one night, correct?"

"That is correct."

"How will you be paying?"

"Cash."

"Would you like to leave a credit card for incidentals?"

"No, thank you. I will leave a cash deposit."

"Very well. I just need to see and ID, and then we're all set."

"Give me a second."

Jaya fumbled in her shoulder bag, almost pulling out her real driver's license. She nervously dropped it back inside and grabbed the Shanice Brooks license. "Here we go, I'm so sorry," she said.

Moments later, Jaya was stepping off the brass elevator on the ninth floor. She walked fast because she had to pee. *Lord, let me get to this room,* she said to herself, trying to hold her legs together. When she got to her room door, she inserted her key card into the slot. A small green light flashed, followed by a beep, and she turned the knob and stepped inside. Dropping her bags at the door, she zoomed into the bathroom.

After Jaya relieved herself, she washed her hands and ran a bath in the Jacuzzi tub. Feeling comfortable, she undressed down to her bra and panties. She went back to the door, got her bags and went into the bedroom. Humming softly, she pulled out her cell phone and dialed Santonio's number. While she waited for him to answer, she parted the curtains and gazed out at the illuminated buildings.

"Hello," Santonio answered.

Jaya could've melted when she heard his voice. A smile spread across her face and she turned and hopped across the bed like a teenage girl, madly in love.

"Hey, baby," she said softly.

"Glad you made it in safely. How is our baby doing?"

Jaya placed her hand on her stomach. She wasn't showing yet, but she knew their baby was in there, and doing exceptionally well. "The baby is fine."

"All right, then."

"But boo, guess what? I saw Puffy downstairs in the lobby and he invited me to an album release party tonight at a club called the Tunnel," she said playfully and waited for Santonio to respond.

He was completely silent.

"I'm just playing," Jaya quickly said.

"Well, I ain't got time to be playing, Jaya." The tone of his voice was cold but relaxed. Almost businesslike. "I'm about to call my people and let him know you're in town. He's gonna come through in about an hour or two. You remember the password?"

"Tony Montana."

"Good, now listen to me. When you get back to Atlanta, there will be a stretch Lincoln Navigator out front to pick you up. The driver already knows what you look like. By tomorrow night, hopefully, we can go ahead and meet your parents in style. When you get in the limo, look inside the bucket of ice. Underneath the ice will be a present for you."

Jaya's heart soared with excitement. "Tell me what's the present."

"It's a surprise, girl. You'll see when you get home, okay?"

"Okay," she said with a pout. Remembering the water running in the in the bathroom, Jaya stood up with the phone still to her ear. "I love you, baby," she said while heading to the bathroom.

"Love you too, baby. Make sure you be careful, and I'll see you tomorrow, okay?"

"Okay," she said and hung up the phone.

Jaya went into the bathroom and turned off the water in the tub. She went back to the bedroom and sat down on the bed. She slowly fell backward, letting her phone fall against the pillows as she stared up at the ceiling. With her eyes closed and her fingers clasped together, she said a silent prayer. *God, I don't know what I would do without you. I knew you would answer my prayers. Thank you so much for bringing Santonio into my life.* She opened her eyes and sat up with a smile. She was happy, joyous, over excited.

Jaya went into the bathroom and removed her underwear, leaving everything in the middle of the floor. When she stepped into the hot water, her body relaxed. She twirled her hair around her fingers and thought, *I want Jagged Edge to sing at my wedding.* Between Santonio and her parents, she was sure it would happen.

Chapter 15

It was nine forty-five when Jaya got her wake-up call from the front desk. "Ok, thank you," she moaned into the phone and dropped her head back down onto the pillow. She didn't feel like moving; it was as if her body had shut completely down. Tucked neatly under the covers, she turned her head and looked at the clock. "I can't believe I slept that long," she said and rubbed her eyes.

Thirty minutes later, she was up and dressed, feeling perky and energetic. Starved, she looked over the room service menu and ordered grilled salmon salad with lemon dill dressing and extra Dijon mustard. Her hair was pulled back in a neat ponytail, and she was dressed in a white bebe t-shirt and sweat pants.

A light knock sounded at the door, causing an adrenaline rush to course through her body. She went to the door, feeling anxious as all outdoors. When she looked through the peephole, she saw a man, but the voice she heard was that of a little boy.

"Look, Daddy, I found it." he said in a slightly Spanish accented voice.

"Who is it?" Jaya asked, never taking her eye away from the peephole.

"Michael," the guy said from the other side.

Michael was who Santonio had told her to expect, but he needed to come with the password before she opened the door. Then, out of the blue, Jaya said in a low tone, "Tony Montana." Her hand flew to her mouth as she realized that she'd made a mistake.

The man on the other side of the door laughed and said, "Yes, that's the correct password, but I think you were supposed to ask me for it."

Jaya pressed her lips together and slowly shook her head. She had messed up. There was nothing to do now but face the music, so she unlocked the door and opened it. In front of her stood the most handsome man that she'd ever seen. She stared at him for a moment. His hair was thick and wavy, and his mustache was neatly trimmed. His sharp brown eyes seemed to look through her. He was dressed in jeans, a leather jacket, and Gucci loafers.

"I messed up, I know," Jaya said as she shook his hand.

"Don't worry, it's nothing important," he responded with a smile.

Jaya relcascd Michael's hand and looked down at the little boy. "And what's your name, handsome?"

The little boy glanced up at her. He had the same features as his father. "I'm big Mike, and my daddy is little Mike," he said and giggled.

Jaya stepped to the side and let them both in

The moment she closed the door, she noticed that Michael was not carrying a bag, which made her curious, but she kept her cool. He went to the sofa and sat down. Little Mike sat down next to him. Jaya noticed that Michael was looking around the room. He got up, walked to the bathroom, and pulled the shower curtain back. It was empty. Next, he checked the closet, which was also empty. Finally, he went into the bedroom and checked the closets and under the bed.

When he returned to the sitting area, Jaya asked, "Is anything wrong?"

Michael shook his head and closed the curtain. "We good, I'm just making sure we're comfortable. Up here, you gotta be on point. You can never be too careful. Niggas in the streets will set you up to get robbed and murdered, or set you up with the Feds. The word, loyalty, doesn't mean much these days, you know."

Jaya listened closely and held on to everything he said. She nodded her head, agreeing with him. "I understand where you coming from, but if you wanna check me for a wire or anything ..." She started to pull the front of her shirt up, but he stopped her.

"I trust you. I'm just the delivery guy, but my people deal straight business. I know you're wondering where the product is, but I got you upstairs in my room. I didn't wanna look out of place. These days, you can't even trust the front desk sometimes."

"Understandable, but what about the money? You ready to count it?"

Michael studied Jaya's body underneath her sweat pants. She was shapely and thick. He picked up the remote and hit the power button. The television would occupy his son while he took care of his business. When the TV came on, a news reporter was reporting live from in front of a high-rise building.

"And just behind me, the Drug Enforcement Agency and ATF have made several arrests in connection with a money laundering, tax evasion, and counterfeit money ring here in Manhattan."

Behind him, federal agents marched a line of people in handcuffs out of the building, including an older man with salt and pepper gray hair, and a younger muscular gentleman with dreads. Micheal studied the TV screen; he did not recognize any of the people arrested. He shrugged and changed the channel.

"Next, on Dragon Ball Z ..." rang from the television.

Little Mike jumped up and pointed. "Look, Daddy, that's Goku."

"Yeah, I see him. I'm Goku and you're Gohan," he said, teasing his son.

Little Mike frowned, then he blurted out, "I'm Goku and you're Gohan, Daddy."

"No, you're wrong ..."

That's when Jaya cleared her throat. "Excuse me, she said with a smile, admiring their father and son relationship. "I don't mean to interrupt this epic battle over cartoons, but I'm ready."

Michael looked Jaya over again. She definitely beautiful, and he wished she would give him some type of sign that they could fuck or something. He had noticed her ring, but that wasn't a factor. Most women wore wedding rings for fashion anyway, he thought.

Jaya set her bag on the table and unzipped it. Michael stepped forward and helped her stack the money in even piles on the table. A knock on the door startled them both. Michael took his hand off the money and reached underneath his jacket to grip his .45 that was tucked in his waist.

"Who is that?" he asked Jaya.

Her eyes met his then went down to his hand resting on the gun. She'd seen that move before, but only on TV. "That's got to be room service," she said.

Jaya moved toward the door and looked through the peephole to confirm. She looked back at Michael and nodded, prompting him to move the money off the table. He sat down in a chair facing the door as Jaya opened it.

A young waiter stood in the threshold with a covered plate on a cart. "Good evening, got your dinner, ma'am."

"Thank you," Jaya said and stepped aside to let him in. "Please put it on the table."

The waiter put the food on the table while Jaya signed the receipt. Michael gave him a twenty-dollar tip, which he gratefully accepted and left the room.

After the waiter left, Michael placed the cash on the table again and began to count. Just as

Jaya was uncovering her plate, Little Mike came up and said, "Daddy, can I have something to eat?"

Michael was focused on counting the money. He looked down at his son, and said, "I'm busy right now. We'll go to White Castle when we leave here."

The little boy stomped his foot. "I don't want White Castle!" He said, and folded his arms.

Jaya couldn't believe the adorable little boy was behaving so badly. "Come on, you can eat with me," she said and reached out for him.

Little Mike walked over to Jaya and stood between her legs. As she fed him, she couldn't help but to think of one day feeding her own son.

Michael thumbed through the money for a few more minutes until he was satisfied that it was all there. He stood up and noticed his son eating with Jaya, and just shook his head, thinking about how spoiled he was. To be fair, he knew that it was past Little Mike's bedtime, and that was most likely the reason for his outburst.

"I'm going upstairs real quick," Michael said to Jaya. He looked at his son. "You wanna go?"

"No." Little Mike snapped.

Michael laughed and told Jaya, "Give me ten minutes and I'll be right back."

Jaya nodded and smiled. "Okay."

Chapter 16

The following morning, Jaya was up early and ready to complete her mission and get home to her man. She was Shanice Brooks again, standing in the mirror, studying herself. Her hair was in a neat ponytail and she wore no makeup. The tired/lazy look is what she was going for. A tired pregnant woman. Jaya wore a girdle, but it had been constructed to conceal the cocaine. She had all four kilos broke down, re-wrapped, and sitting in pockets that had been built into the stomach portion of her girdle. Additional compartments lined the legs of the long line undergarment. Cocaine was stuffed inside those as well. Her hips and ass appeared a bit more plump, definitely enhancing the plain young mother look.

Jaya pulled the large maternity shirt over her head and stepped into a pair of loose fitting jeans. She slid on a pair of wire-rimmed glasses and then put on a thin windbreaker overcoat. Finally satisfied with her look, Jaya gathered her belongings and left the room.

In the lobby, Jaya checked out of the hotel and the doorman hailed a cab to take her to the airport.

———————

The morning was crisp and chilly as Jaya stepped out of the cab at LaGuardia. She hurried into the airport with her carry-on bags and headed directly to the security checkpoint. As she waited in line, Jaya pulled out her phone and called Santonio. He answered on the first ring.

"Hey, what up, baby? You in Atlanta already?"

"No, silly. I'm on the way, though. My flight leaves in forty-five minutes."

"So ... I was thinking ..."

Jaya waited for him to finish, but he was still quiet. "Thinking about what?" she prompted.

"About Maxwell singing at our wedding. I mean, if we gonna do it, we might as well do it big."

Jaya swooned at the thought of Maxwell singing "Fortunate" as she walked down the aisle. She snapped back to reality and said into the phone, "You about to make me cry." The line had moved, and Jaya noticed that she was almost up to the x-ray machine. "I gotta go, baby, it's almost my turn to go through security. You better be in that limo waiting for me when I land."

"I will," he said.

"See you in a little while."

Jaya ended the call with a huge smile on her face and handed her boarding pass and ID to the TSA agent. As she moved to the x-ray table, she visualized herself walking down the center aisle in a huge church, dressed in a snow white wedding gown. Her stepfather escorted her in an all-white tuxedo, with two little girls leading the way to the altar, dropping rose petals on the burgundy carpet. The pews were filled on each side; some of her associates from school were there, along with numerous family and friends. Santonio was standing next to the pastor, definitely handsome in his cream colored tuxedo with a long tail jacket. Her mother smiled at her from the front row.

Cameras flashed and videographers shuffled for position to capture them as they moved.

Jaya was thinking that their honeymoon would be in the Bahamas or maybe Brazil, when she heard, "Excuse me, ma'am?"

Jaya blinked to get her bearings and quickly placed her bags in an x-ray bin. That's when she noticed the airport security guard standing in front of her along with two other gentlemen. One was the security supervisor, a mean looking white man in a white shirted uniform, with a gold badge on the chest.

Jaya didn't know if she was busted, or if this was part of a routine protocol. Her heart thumped rapidly in her chest, but she didn't panic until she saw two men in DEA jackets coming toward her with muzzled K-9 German Shepherds.

She turned toward the security guard. "What can I do for you?"

"Ma'am, please step out of line and come with us."

"Miss, I'm pregnant ..."

The dogs began to bark and strain against their leashes. They seemed to be trying to reach Jaya. She looked around nervously, praying for a miracle. The other passengers had started to notice the commotion and were pointing and whispering. Jaya felt dizzy. *This can't be happening,* she thought, as the police led her down a wide corridor with bright fluorescent lights and took her inside a small room.

Two white female officers were waiting for her when she entered. One of them instructed her to strip.

"I'm not taking my clothes off in front of you," Jaya firmly stated.

"Ma'am," one of them said. "You can strip for us or you can strip for the DEA. The choice is yours."

Jaya stood there, her eyes cold as ice. She looked from one of them to the other. Santonio was going to be pissed, but she knew he would take care of everything. *He always comes through, and plus, I got his baby. He'll come and get us.* Jaya told herself calmly.

Book 3
Jaya and Joi

Chapter 17

A foul stench filled Jaya's nose when she stepped out of the federal transport van into the underground garage at the Metropolitan Correctional Center in Manhattan. This was the holding facility for male and female prisoners who were detained by the Feds. Jaya was shackled at her ankles and handcuffed in front. Two US Marshals had accompanied her from the airport, a female and a male.

The male officer knelt down in front of Jaya and removed her leg irons. Jaya looked around the strange place, depressed and angry all at once. The smell of mildew infiltrated her nose and turned her stomach. *My baby!* She said to herself.

"This way, ma'am," the female officer said, and touched Jaya on the back of her arm.

They led her through a thick electronic door and up a short flight of stairs. The officers were talking amongst themselves, but Jaya wasn't paying them any attention. All she knew was that she'd just been caught red-handed with four kilos of cocaine, and just thinking about it made her start sweating. *Keep calm, Jaya,* she told herself. *Santonio will handle everything. The wedding is still in progress. I wonder if somebody set me up like in the movies. Jesus, my mother is going to have a fit.*

Jaya thought about her mother's advice concerning a man and his shoes. "Fuck his shoes," she mumbled.

"Excuse me?" the male US Marshal questioned.

Jaya looked up at him, thought about what she said, then in a dry tone, she answered, "Nothing, just thinking out loud."

They took Jaya up to an open area with a four-foot high counter. Cameras were in every corner, and behind the desk were more federal agents, some sitting behind the counter, and some were standing around looking at paperwork. Phones were buzzing like crazy. Jaya looked around at the unfamiliar scene as the female marshal removed her handcuffs. If her situation weren't so dire, all of the activity would have fascinated her.

A tall, white female officer walked up to them. "When she gets the cuffs off you, I'm gonna need you to stand over there on a set of those yellow footprints, ok?"

Jaya looked to her right where the lady was pointing and saw yellow footprints. She nodded as she rubbed her wrists after the cuffs were off.

"I need a nice, pretty picture."

Jaya turned up her nose at the smart mouthed matron, then she walked over to the footprints and faced the camera. The camera flashed and Jaya frowned.

"Ok, turn to your left."

Not thinking, Jaya turned to her right.

"Your other left," the lady shouted with a chuckle. "I see why you got caught," she added.

That statement made Jaya mad, but she didn't respond. She simply turned the other way. The camera flashed again. Jaya looked at the lady. "May I please make a phone call?"

"After we get you fingerprinted, darling. It's no need to hurry, you have a few questions to answer first anyway."

"Hmph." Jaya grunted and rolled her eyes.

Moments later, they led Jaya inside an office with a nice shiny cherry wood desk sitting near the back wall. A white man was behind the desk, dressed in a blue two piece suit, white shirt, and a nice tie. The Marshals escorted Jaya in and left.

The man stood up and walked around the desk. He gave Jaya his hand first, and then he showed her his badge.

As soon as Jaya read the letters, DEA, she knew what she was about to go through.

"I'm Federal Agent Miles." He shook her hand briefly. "Good morning."

"Good morning," she said, returning his greeting with sweaty palms.

Miles walked back around the desk, and Jaya watched him as he looked down at something, and then back up to her. "I have a couple of questions that I would like to ask you."

In a split second, Jaya remembered a TV show that was similar to her current situation. She was just about to respond when the agent spoke again.

"You live in Atlanta?"

"Yes ... sir. Umm, I don't want to answer any questions until I can speak with my parents."

Miles studied her for a moment. He came around, sat on the edge of his desk, and folded his arms across his chest. In a calm tone, he said, "You got caught coming through the airport with over four thousand grams of cocaine, Miss Woods, and you're a pregnant college student at

Spelman. From what I've heard about Spelman, it is an excellent school, so I know you're not stupid." He paused; his eyes were dead on hers. From the way he delivered his words, she could tell that he expected a response.

Instead, Jaya's eyes teared up and she said, "Sir, I just wanna call home."

"And you will, but calling home isn't going to get you home, Ms. Woods." He slowly dropped his head and shook it from side to side, then he looked back up at her. "I'm sure you really don't understand." He produced a card with his name and number on it and handed it to Jaya.

Jaya took the card and swallowed hard. Her throat was dry, and she felt so out of place that her body had become numb.

"If you change your mind and decide to help yourself, all you have to do it call," he said and pressed a button on his desk phone. "She's ready," Miles said into the intercom.

A few seconds later, the female marshal came back in and led Jaya out of the office.

Two hours had passed since her arrest, and now Jaya was outfitted in a loose fitting two piece green jumper. They had her sitting on a small bench with her back against the wall, waiting to complete processing along with several other female detainees. Jaya was tired, and she still hadn't used the phone, but at least she was in line. I've got to get out of this place, she thought to herself. When she stood up, an officer led her down a long corridor where a dozen other women were lined up and down the walls. Ahead of them were six pay phones, all occupied.

When Jaya spotted the phones, it was almost like water in the middle of the Sahara desert. She fell in line, put her back against the wall, folded her arms across her chest, and waited. The other female prisoners chatted among themselves, but Jaya paid them no mind. Her patience was running short on her wait. Five minutes turned to ten, and then ten to twenty. When thirty minutes passed, Jaya became aggravated. She needed to speak with Santonio so bad, that she was becoming sick to her stomach.

Jaya stepped out of the line and started making her way toward the front. She passed at least six women who were waiting to use the phone as well, when out of nowhere, a voice yelled out, "And where the fuck you think you going?"

Jaya paused in her tracks, turned and scanned the line of females to see where the disrespectful voice had come from. When she made eye contact with the yellow female who had come out of the line with her hand on her hip, she'd already figured it was her.

"Excuse me?" Jaya said with a cocky attitude.

"Bitch, you heard what the fuck I said," Joi snapped angrily. "Can't you see it's a fuckin' line?" Her voice was high pitched, and her New York accent made it even higher.

That was just enough to push Jaya over the edge. She bit down on her bottom lip, and her eyes turned cold and deadly. "I got ya bitch. Bitch!"

Jaya rushed toward Joi, and Joi met her half way. They both began throwing blows, neither landing a single punch. Jaya grabbed Joi by the front of her shirt and pushed her up against the wall. Joi grabbed Jaya by her ponytail and yanked her head backward.

Another female yelled from the side, "Beat that country bitch's ass!"

Jaya was stronger, but she was breathing harder. She put her fingernails in Joi's neck and drew blood.

Whistles pierced the air as three matrons came running down the hall, screaming, "Everybody face the wall! Face the wall!"

They separated Jaya and Joy, then another tall, black female sergeant approached and asked, "What the fuck is the problem, here?"

Jaya was beyond angry. Her chest rose and fell with each labored breath as she tried to get a hold of herself. Joi was trying to keep calm, but she was live wire with an ill temper. They both continued to bicker. "This bitch this, and this bitch that," was all that anyone could make out of the argument.

"Shut the fuck up!" the matron yelled at both of them. "Turn around, hands against the wall, both of y'all."

The two women turned around and placed the palms of their hands against the walls, glaring at each other the whole time. The matron said to one of the other guards, "Give me a set of cuffs."

Joi took her hands off the wall and turned around. "Look, I don't know this chick. We were arguing over the phone. That's it."

"Turn around and face the wall. Do NOT take your hands off the wall again unless I tell you to."

The tall officer with the handcuffs pulled Jaya's right hand and cuffed her to Joi's left hand. They both looked around and couldn't believe what was happening. They had no idea what was going on.

The matron pointed at Jaya. "Name?"

"Jaya Woods."

"Name?" she said to Joi.

"Joi Davis," she said in a cocky tone.

"Ok, Ms. Woods and Ms. Davis, I'm going to place both of you in holding cell six and let you get better acquainted for a couple of hours while you cool off."

Joy's face fell. "Excuse me, ma'am, but I really need to make a phone call."

"You had your chance for that, Ms. Woods." She looked at her wristwatch. "We'll see how it goes at around one or one thirty."

"One or one thirty!" Jaya and Joi repeated in unison.

This angered the matron even more. "Better yet, let's make that four o'clock this evening," she said.

Neither girl said anything else after that. They knew if they went any further, they might lose the chance to make a call for the entire day.

Another matron pulled out her radio and spoke into it. "Main control, open cell six, second floor, please."

The matrons escorted the handcuffed girls down the hall and to the right. When they reached cell six, she motioned for them to step in.

Joi and Jaya entered the cell one behind the other, still handcuffed together.

The matron smirked and said, "And if you two decide to become a little more ... um, how shall I put this? Acquainted ... let me know so I can watch." A smile spread across her face, then she pulled her radio up to her mouth. "Main control, close cell six, please." She stepped back, and the steel door closed automatically.

Inside the cold cell, Jaya and Joi stood still, looking confused by the matron's statement, and perplexed about why they were still handcuffed together. They had no choice but to play nice.

The cell had a high twelve-foot ceiling, and a metal bench that spanned two walls, forming an L shape. The floor was covered wall to wall with a gray indoor-outdoor carpet. In the right corner was a stainless steel toilet and sink attached to each other, with a square mirror that had the words, FUCK THE FEDS engraved into it.

Joi and Jaya looked around in disbelief. Neither could believe the situation that they were in. "We might as well sit down," Joi said, and then she breathed heavily and shook her head.

The air blowing in the cell felt about fifty degrees. "It's cold as shit in here," Joi said and shivered.

Jaya nodded in agreement, but she wasn't really up for any small talk. The only thing on her mind was getting to the phone and calling Santonio and her mother.

They sat quietly for a few moments and then, Jaya finally asked, "You been here before?"

Joi looked over at Jaya. Her eyes were tired. "Hell no," she responded. "This is my first time being locked up, ever."

"Wow, me too," Jaya said, then she added, "I don't have the slightest clue as to what is going on."

"What they bring you in for?"

"Four kilos of cocaine. I was at the airport."

"Damn! So you were a mule?" Joi asked.

"A mule?"

Yeah, a mule is someone that goes state to state to pick up the dope for whoever you're working for."

Jaya sat quietly for a couple of minutes, pondering Joi's last statement. It didn't sound right to her. "Nah, I was taking trips for my fiancé. We're about to get married, and I am carrying his baby."

"So, you preggo right now? Congratulations, even under the circumstances. Now I see why you were vexed about getting to that phone."

"Thanks, and yeah, I got a lot of shit going on."

"Well, whatever you do, don't tell them bitches shit. I mean, nothing at all. Wait until you talk to your people. And don't call and say anything over the phone. That'll get your people fucked up too. They record all the phone calls."

"Man, I'm glad you said that." Jaya's mind was racing in several directions again, feeling as if she was about to lose her mind. She was stressing more and more by the minute. "What they get you for?" she asked Joi.

Joi laughed halfheartedly, looked at Jaya, and said, "Well, according to the indictment, it's money laundering and racketeering. But I got a weak ass case."

"How you know it's weak?" Jaya asked.

Joi leaned toward Joi and whispered in her ear, "Because the key witness in my case is dead."

Chapter 18

At Hartsfield-Jackson International, Santonio sat in the rear of the parked Navigator limousine playing a one on one game of NBA Live on PlayStation. The TV in the limousine was small, but he was just passing time because the flight was late. Hell, American did fuck up every now and then. Santonio looked at his watch. It was almost noon, and Jaya should've come through the door at least an hour ago. He paused his game and tapped the partition.

The driver lowered the glass immediately and looked back at Santonio. "Yes, sir?"

"Can you go inside and see if the flight from LaGuardia got in yet?"

"Sure, I'll look for your fiancé as well," he said and stepped out.

Santonio felt that something wasn't right, he just didn't know what it was. His cell phone lay on the leather seat next to him. Santonio picked it up and punched in Jaya's number. It rang once, then went to voicemail. He hung up and dialed her again. Same thing. *She must be in the air,* he thought. *Got to be.*

Santonio looked at his watch again. Two minutes passed, then he opened the door and stepped outside. The fresh air rushed him. He scanned the area then leaned against the hood of the limo, holding his phone in his hand, just in case Jaya called.

People continuously walked in and out of the airport, and Santonio studied them all. A slender brown-skinned chick pulling her suitcase behind her passed him. He immediately thought about Jaya and dialed her number again. When the voicemail came on for the third time, he simply said, "Call me."

Ten more minutes went by, according to his watch, before the limousine driver headed back toward him. Santonio tried to read body language and facial expression before he got to him.

"The plane landed forty-five minutes ago," the driver said.

Santonio said nothing. He checked his watch once again to cover his growing panic. Something was really wrong. He took a deep breath and looked the driver in the eyes. Santonio couldn't even speak to him about the situation because he didn't want to put a stranger in his business.

"Sit tight," he said to the driver. "Let me make a couple of calls."

The driver nodded and hopped into the front seat.

Santonio sighed and dialed his ex-girlfriend's number. She answered on the first ring.

"Hey Sweetheart," she said. Her voice was soft and innocent, unlike the demanding tone she had used just a day before. She actually sounded happy to hear from him.

"Look, do me a favor. Call your girl at American Airlines and see if Shanice Brooks boarded flight 1890 from LaGuardia to Atlanta. It came in at eleven forty-five."

"What's wrong, Santonio?"

Santonio wasn't up for the small talk, he knew that she was the only person that he could talk to about his situation. She did sound concerned, so Santonio took a deep breath, feeling himself sweating under his shirt and said, "I'm at the airport. Shawty was supposed to land an hour ago, and she hasn't shown up."

"Well, don't start worrying. Let me call up there, and I'll call you back in ten minutes."

"Where you at?" he asked. His nerves were frayed as he walked back to the limousine and climbed inside.

"I'm home. Why don't you come over?"

Santonio was easily swayed by her words. "Well, call me back and let me know what the business is."

"Okay, give me a few minutes," she said and hung up.

Santonio took the bottle of Cristal from the bucket, popped the top, and turned it up, hoping it would ease his pain.

It didn't work.

In the ten minutes that he waited for Shannon to call him back, he'd drunk half the bottle of champagne. His phone rang and he jumped, nervous because he could feel the bad news.

"Wuss'up?" was all he said.

"She jammed up, baby."

Santonio's entire body slumped, just like a deflated tire. "Who got her? State or Fed?"

"Feds. She never made it past LaGuardia."

"Fuck ... shit!" he yelled. He was thirty-eight hot. That was his last dollar, and now, Jaya was locked up.

"Come over here, Santonio."

Santonio was lost in thought. He felt like his entire world had crumbled. His heart threatened to beat out of his chest, and he was sweating like a hooker in church.

"Yo," Santonio said to the driver. "Change of plans. We won't be going to dinner this evening. Please take me back home."

"Yes, sir," the driver responded, and started the limousine.

———————

Two hours later, Santonio arrived at the estate in Guillford Forrest in the rental car that he had picked up a couple days before. He reluctantly parked in front of the garage. It was awkward for him to be back there since he'd ended his relationship with Shannon to be with Jaya. He'd moved all of his clothes out, and was preparing to move into another place in Peachtree City. Now, he didn't know what his next move would be.

When Santonio got out the car, Shannon was already waiting for him at the front door in a short t-shirt and thin yoga pants. The first thing she did was wrap her arms around his waist and bury her face in his chest. Santonio needed that hug. Truth be told, there were lingering feelings on both sides, but hers were just stronger than his.

"Come on in," she said and pulled him into the foyer.

Santonio walked in, and couldn't help but to admire Shannon's nicely shaped body as he walked behind her. Inside the living room, which featured a tray ceiling, Santonio sat down on the thick cushioned loveseat, and Shannon sat next to him.

She turned her body toward Santonio and took his hand in hers. "Did she have everything?"

Another long sigh escaped from Santonio, then he threw his head backward and looked up at the ceiling. He was beyond stressed. "I sent her to get four keys with my last dollar."

Shannon put her hand under Santonio's shirt and rubbed his chest. "Baby, you should know that money isn't an issue. Don't stress yourself about that. I have a hundred thousand that I can turn into cash if you need it." She moved in closer and said, "I just don't want you to leave me again, baby."

Santonio's brain woke up when she said she had a hundred thousand dollars that she could turn into cash for him. It sounded good as hell. However, he knew that she was too arrogant and stuck on herself to just give in that easily. Her selfish nature was one of the reasons they broke up. However, he had a major situation with Jaya being locked up. He didn't know if she had called his name or rolled on him, as most women did when faced with this situation.

"I just can't leave her in there like that," Santonio said.

Shannon kissed the side of his face. "I understand, baby, and whatever you decide, I'm with you for the long run. Now, I'm gonna fill the Jacuzzi up with some hot water, I'm gonna give you a massage from head to toe, and then I'm going to cook you dinner. But first, I want you to relax for a moment."

She reached for his zipper, worked his soft dick out of his pee hole, and massaged it. Then, she got down on her knees between his legs and wrapped her mouth around the head of his dick.

Already feeling more relaxed, Santonio leaned up, put his phone and keys on the table, and got comfortable.

Chapter 19

After a few hours had passed, Joi was out cold. Jaya nudged her arm. They were both cold and had nearly huddled together, just to keep warm.

Joi batted her eyes open and looked up at Jaya. "What's up?"

"Hate to wake you, but I got to pee," Jaya said.

Sounds good to me, 'cause I got to pee too."

They stood up together and stretched, then they went over to the toilet, having to do everything together. Jaya rolled off some tissue and spread it around the toilet. Joi turned her back while Jaya relieved herself, and then Jaya returned the favor for Joi. A few minutes later, they were both done. Together, they washed their hands, before returning to the bench.

For the next hour, they talked, sharing college stories and details of their lives growing up. They realized that they had so much in common. Joi was a bit more street smart than Jaya, and she put her up on a lot of game. They both were in bad situations and had to wait for the outcome.

"And what's up with this man talking ass bitch?" Joi asked, referring to the tall matron officer.

Jaya laughed and added, "If we decide to keep each other company, to let her know so she can watch." She looked at Joi. "That bitch got some nerves, right?"

Someone tapped on the glass of the cell door and the girls stood up in unison. "They must be ready to let us out of here, Jaya said.

The door slid open as they were walking toward it. A short chubby female dressed in a white top and matching bottoms, wearing a hairnet and gloves walked in. She was very unattractive, with big feet and pushed a small metal cart with two Styrofoam trays on it. "It's lunch time, ladies," she said.

A female officer stood behind her.

"How are we supposed to eat cuffed together?" Jaya asked.

The female officer pulled out her keys and said, "If you be patient, big mouth, I'm about to take them off."

Jaya and Joi both stood there shaking their heads in silence. The smart talking and disrespect was driving them both crazy.

After the officer removed the cuff, Joi said, "Can you bring me a few alcohol pads for my neck?"

The lady looked at Joi's neck. "It's only a scratch. I'll see what I can do."

When the inmate handed them their trays, she also gave them each a styrofoam cup filled with lemonade.

The door started to close again, and Jaya asked before it closed, "What about our phone time?"

The door closed in her face.

Joi yelled, "What about our dessert then, bitch?" She was angry, and they were really beginning to think that they would not get to use the phone at all.

The two young ladies sat back down on the bench next to each other and opened their trays. Lunch looked good. They had hot spaghetti with ground turkey, garden salad, garlic bread, and a half ear of corn, with a small cup of butter and salad dressing. They ate together and talked some more. Time came and went, and then dinner was served, but still, no phone.

Five thirty the following morning, the door opened. Jaya and Joi were both sleeping in uncomfortable positions. "Phone," the tall lady said.

Jaya wiped her eyes, at first, not realizing where she was. Then it hit her like a ton of bricks. She tapped Joi and woke her up. "They about to let us use the phone."

Joi hopped up and looked toward the open door. She followed Jaya out into the corridor, and the matron led them to the phones. "Fifteen minutes," she told them. "Y'all got court this morning."

––––––––

Santonio was in a deep, peaceful sleep in his king sized bed, tucked between the sheets, snuggled up behind Shannon when his cell phone rang on the nightstand. He turned over immediately and picked it up. The number was unfamiliar, but something told him to answer it anyway.

"Hello," he said.

"Santonio?" a female voice asked.

He didn't recognize the voice. "Yes, this me," he said cautiously.

"This is Karen, Jaya's mother. She's on the other line, and I'm about to click her on."

Santonio felt butterflies in his stomach. He sat up a little more in the bed and cleared his throat, trying to prepare himself for the phone conversation.

Jaya came on the line. "Hey, baby," she said softly. Her voice sounded sad and worried.

Santonio took another deep breath. He knew he couldn't say too much because her mother was on the phone listening, and so was the Feds.

"My daughter is locked up and pregnant, now what are you gonna do about it?

"Mama, I can speak for myself," Jaya interrupted. "Santonio, baby, can you come get me out?" Jaya asked like it was just that easy.

"Have you had a bond hearing yet?" Santonio asked then looked over at Shannon. Her eyes were on him, taking in every word he spoke.

Santonio pointed to his crotch, and Shannon moved her mouth down to his dick and began to give him what he wanted.

"I'm supposed to be going to court in a few minutes," she said.

Santonio could hear her crying although she was trying to be brave. He looked down at

Shannon. She had half of his dick down her throat, and it was feeling too damn good. He had his left hand on the back of her head, as he said into the phone, "Let's see what they say. Can you call me back when you come out of court?"

"I don't ... don't know. I ... I don't wanna be here."

Santonio just listened to her cry. There was nothing he could do at this point, but try to convince her not to say anything about him. Shannon was sucking his dick so good, that he had to look down at her again. She stared up at him, holding his dick with both hands. Her job was to keep her man occupied and to keep him from stressing about Jaya.

"Call me back at four oh four, seven nine three, two eight three seven."

"Okay, I got it. Love you, baby."

"Love you too," Santonio said and hung up.

He placed the phone back on the nightstand and placed both hands behind his head, trying his best to relax.

"Do it feel good, baby?" she asked him.

Santonio closed his eyes and said, "Hell yeah, don't stop."

Chapter 20

"You've thrown your life away on a nothing ass negro," Karen said after Santonio hung up.

Tears streamed down Jaya's face as she said, "He gonna get me out, Mama."

"Oh really?" Karen said angrily. "How?"

Jaya had no answer.

"What are your charges?"

"I was trafficking four grams of cocaine."

Karen was quiet for a moment. Jaya knew that she was beyond pissed. "Let me make some calls. When you go to court, plead not guilty until I get a lawyer to come see you. Call me as soon as you get back."

Jaya hung up the phone and wiped her face on her t-shirt. She looked over at Joi on the other phone. She seemed so calm and in control. Jaya wished she was strong like Joi was, but she knew that everyone was different, and no one handled everything the same way.

Joi slammed the phone down and yelled, "These bitches froze all of my accounts!" She turned to see Jaya staring at her. "You good, ma?" she asked.

Jaya shrugged. "I guess."

An hour later, Jaya was underground. She was shackled around her ankles, chained at her waist, and cuffed around her wrists. Two male officers escorted her as she hop/marched through a tunnel nearly forty feet below the city. She was nervous and very uncomfortable as she thought about her mother, Santonio, her unborn baby, and wondered if she'd ever see Joi again. Jaya went through a maze of corridors with electronic doors at each end, which were operated remotely by officers watching her entire journey on surveillance cameras.

When Jaya and her escorts reached the North end of the tunnel, they waited for the prisoner elevator to take them up to the courthouse. While Jaya waited, she thought to herself, *they got me going through these tunnels like I'm a terrorist or something.* Nearly another hour passed while Jaya waited inside another holding tank to see the judge. Breakfast was served on another Styrofoam tray. Scrambled eggs, turkey bacon,

French toast, and orange juice. This morning, she had no appetite whatsoever. Too much bullshit was going through her head. It seemed that she'd been waiting an entire day, and time was still running.

At nine thirty am, Jaya finally stepped inside the courtroom for her hearing. It was quiet, with only a few people standing around and scattered in the pews. The judge sat up front; he wasn't old and fat like Jaya expected him to be. This guy was slim, with a strong chin, black hair, and wire-framed glasses. Nevertheless, he was still wearing the black robe.

As Jaya waited for the proceedings to begin, a woman came through the courtroom doors. It seemed that the entire room turned and looked in her direction. Jaya stared at her as well, because she had entered like she owned the place. She was tall, probably six feet or better in her heels, and extraordinarily beautiful. Her long wavy hair was pinned up, her eyes were slanted, and her skin was a creamy brown. She walked like a professional model in her dark green two-piece casual pantsuit, carrying a leather briefcase with a long pink scarf around her neck.

AKA, Jaya immediately thought upon seeing the pink and green. She got nervous when the stunning woman walked over to her and wondered what she wanted.

"I'm Amanda Ross," she said. "Your mother and I are good friends."

Jaya shook Amanda's hand and smiled for the first time since this nightmare began. "Good morning, I'm Jaya Woods."

Both US Marshals hover over Jaya. One of them asked, "Are you her attorney?"

Amanda turned her head and looked dead in his ice blue eyes. "Yes, I am." Then she rolled her eyes at him and turned up her nose.

Amanda Ross was a criminal defense attorney with an impressive track record in federal court. She'd won several high profile criminal cases with charges ranging from Rico offenses, murder, armed robbery, and trafficking. She laid it on the line for her clients, which was why she was so popular. A few years before, she had almost lost her license after she attempted to sleep with a judge to get her rich client off a conspiracy charge.

"May I have a word with my client alone for a minute?" Amanda asked the Marshals.

When they walked off, Amanda watched to see how far they'd go. It was only about five yards, but definitely out of earshot. She glanced up at the judge to see if he was ready, but he wasn't.

The judge was holding a conversation with the DA.

Amada turned to Jaya. "Your mother called me as soon as she got off the phone with you, and she's pissed."

"You came from Atlanta that fast?"

"No, New Jersey. I'm licensed in New Jersey and New York, but I live in Jersey." Amanda said as she pulled a pen and pad from her briefcase.

"Can you get me out?" Jaya asked anxiously. She wasn't thinking about anything else but her freedom.

Amanda pulled out a pair of glasses and slipped them on her face. She looked at Jaya and said, "I'm not trying to alarm you or anything, but it's gonna be an uphill battle. By you being from out of state, the DA will probably say that you're a flight risk and try to refuse bail, or set it at a ridiculous price like a million or two. You never know with these people. Plus, they hate me up here." She paused and smiled. "But it's a good hate. Tell me about yourself," Amanda said as she put the pen against the notepad.

For the next fifteen minutes, Jaya and Amanda went back and forth, with questions and answers. Amanda asked Joi about Santonio, and she tried to explain as much as possible.

"Have you said anything to anyone about your case?"

Jaya hesitated and thought about her conversations with Joi back in the holding tank. "Yes, I got into a fight with a girl named Joi Davis, and we were placed in the tank together. I told her what I was locked up for, and she told me not to say anything to anyone over the phone until I had a lawyer."

"Well, she did tell you right, however, don't discuss your business with anyone."

Amanda scribbled Joi Davis' name down on the notepad for safe keeping. She was about to ask Jaya another question when the bailiff's voice interrupted her. "All rise."

Amanda tapped Jaya on the arm for her to stand. She stood up next to Amanda and felt her hands tremble a bit. The judge waved his hand dismissively, as if to tell the few people in the courtroom to relax. He looked down at some paperwork for a moment before looking over at Jaya and Amanda Ross.

"Ms. Ross, good morning."

Amanda nodded, smiled, and said, "Good morning, sir." Amanda knew the judge very well. When he was a DA, she'd beaten him once in court and lost to him twice.

"Are you representing this young lady in the trafficking case?" he asked Amanda.

"Yes, sir, I am. And—"

The judge held up his hand. "Hold on, I know you're ready to out talk me. Just hold your horses."

Amanda smiled at him, but on the inside, she was heated. She didn't like when a Judge tried to shine on her, especially in a courtroom. But, she knew how to play her position. The judge looked at Jaya for a brief moment, and then back down at his paperwork. "Miss Woods, good morning," he said, peering at her over the top of his glasses.

"Good morning, your honor."

"You're a student at Spelman College in Atlanta, correct?"

Jaya nodded. "Yes, I am."

The judge shook his head and took a deep breath. "Why do you young ladies waste your parents' hard earned money sending you to these great schools, only to throw it all away?

Jaya just stood there, lost for words. At that moment, she wished she'd never met Santonio, but then she thought about her unborn child and wished that this was all a dream. Jaya dropped her head as her eyes moistened. She was on the verge of breaking down.

"Your honor, may I approach the bench?" Amanda asked.

She was already walking toward him before he could respond. When she got close enough to speak privately, she said, "Sir, my client is pregnant, and I was hoping that you would set a reasonable bond."

The judge's eyes were on Amanda. He smiled and nodded at her, and then she walked back over to the defense table. Jaya was still crying, with her face now buried in her hands.

"Cash only bond to be set at one point five million dollars," the judge said and pounded the gavel.

"Are you kidding me?" Amanda blurted out.

The judge stood and banged the gavel again, and without another word, he exited the courtroom.

Amanda couldn't believe what had just happened. She felt low and defeated as the two marshals came over to take Jaya back.

"Give me five minutes, please."

Jaya was crushed. She really believed that everything would be all right, and she would be able to go home.

"Shh," Amanda said. "Listen to me." She lifted Jaya's face so she could look at her.

Jaya's eyes were red, and quickly turning puffy. She wiped her eyes with the back of her hand and looked at Amanda. "I can't have my baby here," she said desperately.

"I'm going do everything in my power to make it possible for you to go home. But you have to be strong for you and your baby, okay? As of right now, nothing else matters." Amanda held Jaya's face between her hands. "Take a deep breath."

Jaya took a deep breath.

"Do it again."

She took another one. Amanda reached over to her briefcase, pulled out a tissue and wiped Jaya's eyes. "Calm yourself down. You're stronger than you could ever imagine, Jaya. I'm here for you, and not against you. Just go with the flow and trust me."

Santonio had told her that same thing. Another memory that she was beginning to hate.

"Give me a few weeks, and we'll try it again. I'm sure I can pull a couple of strings.

Jaya nodded.

Amanda gave Jaya her business card with her cell number, home and office number on it. She reminded her not to discuss her case with anyone, but Jaya didn't know if she could hold to that. Joi was her friend, and the only person she felt that she could talk to.

When Amanda and Jaya departed, Amanda smiled, extended her pinky finger, and made a motion as she said, "Skee ... Wee."

Chapter 21

Santonio stood in the shower, allowing the hot water to beat against his body and massage his skin. His Armani soap had the entire bathroom smelling good. He was in deep thought about Jaya, her parents, their baby, and the wedding they were planning. It all made him shake his head in disgust. He had fallen in love with someone he had no business falling in love with, and now he was caught between a rock and a hard place.

Shannon peeked her head in. "Breakfast is waiting," was all she said.

From the glass shower, he looked at her and said, "I'll be out in a minute."

Santonio had to regroup. He needed to get this money from Shannon, and if he needed to, he would catch him another young female to go get the work for him again. He rinsed off and turned off the water.

In the den, Shannon was wiping off the table with a dust cloth when the phone rang.

"Hello," she answered.

""Umm, is Santonio there?" Jaya asked.

Shannon looked around to make sure that she was alone. She didn't want Santonio to walk up on her while she was on the phone, so she walked outside onto the rear patio and closed the door behind her. "Listen," she said into the phone. "I don't know who you are or what the situation is, but Santonio is my man. He's left town because he thinks you're gonna put his name in your case. Now, I don't know your situation or what dealings you had with him, but he's gone now, and I would advise you to lose this number." She hung up before Jaya could utter one word.

Shannon walked back into the house and went to the kitchen. Santonio was sitting on one of the four stools at the bar, wrapped in a cozy Gucci robe. She walked up behind him, wrapped her arms around his neck and kissed his cheek. "After we eat, we're going to the bank," she said.

Santonio turned his head and kissed her lips with passion. She massaged his neck a little bit, and then went to the stove, which sat on the kitchen island.

Shannon was very health conscious, so breakfast consisted of lean turkey bacon, an egg white omelet and toasted wheat bread for him. She had a half grapefruit and Special K cereal.

As they ate, all Santonio could think about was the money. He needed it like he needed his next breath.

After they ate, Shannon stood up and said, "Get dressed, baby, so we can go. You know how the Atlanta traffic is."

Santonio stood up and wrapped his arms around her waist. "All right," he said and kissed her lips before heading toward the bedroom.

Once Santonio was gone, Shannon picked up her phone and dialed a number while walking toward the rear of the house.

"US Attorney's office, this is Bill. How may I help you?"

"Hello, Bill," this is Shannon. I called you a couple days ago with the information about the Shanice Brooks girl. I was just wondering if everything went okay?"

"Yes, yes, Shannon, how are you? Sorry, I didn't get back with you, but everything went well. We have her in custody. Thank you so much for all your help."

"Thank you, Bill. Good day and God bless."

Shannon hung up the phone and joy coursed through her body. "You ready, boo?" she called out to Antonio.

"I'm coming," Santonio yelled back.

Jaya dropped the phone in shock after the devastating phone call that she had just completed. Her entire body seemed to have locked up. Feeling dizzy, she leaned against the wall. The corridor started to spin.

"Girl, what's wrong with you?" a voice asked.

Jaya could hear the sound, but the words did not register. The lights in the ceiling spun around, the walls seemed to open and close, almost as if they were breathing. Her stomach did the same. Jaya stumbled, gagged, and then vomited all over herself and the floor. This wasn't good at all.

An emergency medical call went out over the PA system. A team of nurses rushed in and loaded Jaya on a gurney. The scene was chaos. Noise, yelling, police telling the other prisoners to face the wall and get out of the way.

Jaya's face was covered with an oxygen mask. She'd gone into shock and had begun to bleed heavily between her legs. The nurses immediately cut her clothes off when they got her to the medical wing. The doctor was ready and waiting for her.

The doctor performed a quick examination of Jaya. "Poor girl," he said to the nurse. "She was pregnant, and just lost her baby."

To Be Continued ...

CPSIA information can be obtained
at www.ICGtesting.com
Printed in the USA
LVHW030045180821
695508LV00006B/991

9 781517 650117